A Storm Within

A Novel

A Storm Within

A Novel

DANIEL HILL ZAFREN

Published by Time Treasures Books, Goose Creek, South Carolina
www.timetreasuresbooks.com

ISBN: 978-1-7345129-2-2

Printed in the United States of America

Cover and interior by Susan Newman Design Inc.

The earlier books by Daniel Hill Zafren:

In a World We Never Made (2001)
A Door Never Opened (2003)
Shadow Selves (2005)
Network of Death (2006)
Not Lost – Just Not Found (2008)
Restless Beauty (2009)
Glimpses of Forgotten Dreams (2010)
Echo in the Heart (2011)
Double Hugs (2011)
Page Passage (2013)
Wish Winds (2014)
Unfinished Thinking (2015)
Vain Regrets (2016)
Network Secret (2016)
Forever Old, Forever New (2017)
Endless Time (2018)
A Gray Voyager (2019)
Right Sight (2020)
Journey to Tomorrow (2020)

Family secrets — dark and deep,
A confidence sworn to keep;
Compromising the keeper as a whole,
A storm within eroding the soul.

Family secrets to be kept or told?
A storm within rages uncontrolled;
A dilemma that continues on
Until the soul is gone.

If a living death is about to begin,
Most certainly it is by a storm within.

Secrets,
running over my soul without sound,
only when dawn comes tip-toeing
ushered by a suave wind,
and dreams disintegrate
like breath shapes in frosty air,
I shall overhear you, barefoot,
scatting off into the darkness....
I shall know you, secrets
by the litter you have left
and by your bloody foot-prints.

Lola Ridge
(1873-1941)

Preface

Young people ask – What will I do with my life? The elderly ask – What have I done with my life? There are no easy answers in either case. The future is basically an unknown, and a large assortment of circumstances may control what, where, and how one proceeds. The past may be filled with facts and objective accomplishments, but a long span of time combined with the human factor such as a strained memory may lead to a degree of uncertainty about such facts. Later thoughts, new and further interpretations, and additional influences can also prompt a changing perception. Further, the young have not had the opportunity to have many regrets, or at least they fail to recognize such until they have aged. The old not only have regrets, perhaps even a slew of them, they can be consumed by them.

It does not seem to make any difference that the old were once young. They did not take full advantage of it then, and now it merely represents missed opportunities as well as things they did not understand and do not see clearly. The young will be old, and there is usually little preparation and scant thought for a stage representing a distant projection and obscure notions. It may seem implausible that instead of controlling events in the later time life will dictate the feasibility of desires. The generation gap is truly a vast wasteland.

The characters an author may conjure up must often cross into the worlds of the young and the old, and the past and future must be handled with reasonable assurance. The present also enters the picture as the necessary and often bewildering bridge between the two worlds. The author also needs to determine for each character whether hindsight or foresight is the stronger motivator taking the character from the present to the future. If the character dreams, so must the author. If the character suffers, so must the author.

In character creation, as in the story that follows, the most compelling and perhaps the most frustrating aspect is when an author establishes one who is designed to be an alter ego. A double life is now lived, that of the author and the character. There might be a tendency to have the latter be the dominant figure because there is greater control and fabricated certainty for the direction and content of events and the interplay with other characters in the life trip. Yet, as a story unfolds, the character actually might control the author. Portrayed actions and events in the grand scheme may have a tendency to seep into the author's conduct and motivations. In a way, it can become living two lives as one even though intended to be separate and apart. It is complicated enough to live but one life. Then, by the story's end, the specter is raised, a philosophical imponderable, of which life is the real one?

One

For Yancy Holister, now an elderly author, each of the twelve novels he had written were mostly involved with the past. Segments of his childhood, familial relations, and personal and world historical events were embellished to establish principles of gentle living immersed in worthwhile endeavors. One aspect he had not dealt with, and one that loomed large in his past, was the presence and handling of disturbing dark secrets. It is undoubtedly true that there are skeletons behind closed doors. Also, few families do not have large and small secrets kept away from prying eyes, perhaps even deep dark secrets that can haunt a person throughout life. It can go beyond that, as it did for Yancy, to become a recurring nightmare. It was a storm within ravaging his soul.

Now that he was old and the meeting of death perhaps imminent, he was the last remaining member of his family that knew about such secrets. A long time burden thrust upon an unwilling and restless recipient. The lengthy harboring of these secrets as well as their content were major factors in who he was. He was certain he would wind up taking these secrets to the grave and the prospect of them dying with him further tore at his soul. More and more in recent times he questioned whether this would be best.

Yancy had no wife to confide in. He had been married twice, both early on and both of a short duration and with an unsatisfactory result. He knew in both instances it was mainly his fault. A writer functions best in a solitary existence. Others, even if close by, can be distractions and considered as trespassers. Their presence can be resented, and subtle objections and annoyances to actions or activities may surface. He was also difficult to live with. He was moody, impatient, and had a bad temper. He shunned social activities unless he knew they were with people who were intellectually challenging, and for that reason had no close friends. Even though he played tennis as a youngster, he had no interest in watching or participating in sports.

There were no children from the marriages, and he often thought he might have enjoyed doting over a child. Even with his shortness of patience and quick temper, he believed he would have been a decent father. There could have been much in the world of ideas that he could have imparted to a little one. Like so many other things that might have been in his life, he merely rationalized that it was not meant to be. Not meant to be is another way of formulating a regret.

It had been nearly ten years since he moved from his rent controlled apartment in Manhattan to the small country home in rural Vermont at the end of a narrow country road. City living had become a drag on his thinking, and he convinced himself that a desolate existence would help him in his writing. So far, that was true, and he also found that he was entranced by living in isolation. The ventures outside to do chores, such as to collect firewood for the wood stove, proved beneficial as they fostered a certain peace with the demons he wrestled with. His thinking was clearer, although he wondered how that was really going to help him in the end. Of course, he fully realized that he could not truly fully escape from himself.

The nearest neighbor he had was George Cosgrove, an older farmer who lived in a huge old clapboard home on a hill with his younger wife, Millie. They were also reclusive which was fine with him. An occasional sighting and even more infrequent greetings were all there was. They were pleasant enough, and he did not expect or want anything more. He did not wish to become close to anyone, and that saved him from conversation and explanations.

He especially enjoyed the isolation during the winter months since nobody came or could come as the road was never plowed. Even the mail was held at the post office in town some thirteen miles away when conditions prevented actual deliveries. He would stock the pantry whenever he went to town, which was not often, and since he was a light eater he seemed to have enough in reserve.

It was the third week in October. Yancy had just put some wood in the wood stove that heated the entire small house. The first heavy snow was falling, and he watched his large mixed breed dog, Chap, short for Chapter, romp around in it. Yancy had adopted the dog from the shelter in town two years earlier although he did not necessarily need a dog. They had told him the dog was about to be euthanized because nobody would adopt him. The two bonded, and Yancy had become rather fond of him. As the snow started to build up he called Chap in the house, dried him off, and then gazed out into the whiteness. The idea came to him as if some voice was calling out to him from the wilderness. He would write a book and the main character would have deep dark secrets, his secrets. Nobody else would guess they were in fact his secrets. A writer's imagination is capable of probing all of the recesses of human emotions and conditions. If any might guess as to their veracity, Yancy would merely emphasize that it was a work of fiction. No further explanations were needed. His publisher would be delighted if the book evoked such speculation. Would he be able to carry it out?

Two

DARK SECRETS
by Yancy Holister

1

He thought walls had secrets. That was because when Casey Trumbeaux was a young boy his family lived in an old tenement building in Brooklyn where the walls between apartments were so thin most sounds and all voices other than hushed whispers could be clearly heard. He knew what was going on in the lives of many of the other families as well as they knew what was going on in his.

His childhood, as he looked back on it and tried to evaluate what it had been, was not marked by any special or extraordinary accomplishment. He grew up street wise, learning more about people and life by observing and listening than any book could teach him. One valuable lesson he learned early on was that people are fascinating and complex creatures with an assortment of strengths and weaknesses, and that some had the capacity to do great deeds of kindness while others might exercise acts of extensive evil. It might very well be difficult to tell in advance which way a person might act or react.

The neighborhood was a mixing bowl of cultures, races, and religions. A natural bond existed with the children crossing all lines and ages, as if they were one family. They all went to the one school in the neighborhood and spent more of their time together than with their home families. It was a given that they were stronger together than apart, and any shock waves were better absorbed in a crowd than individually. There were so many common elements in their daily existence that any differences in skin color, language, or religious practices could not produce any lasting intolerance. Too bad those kinds of lessons and practices could not be expanded to the national and international levels.

The neighborhood was a living diorama of news, gossip, and opinion. It did not take long for one growing up to learn there were secrets and then there were secrets. Once a story became common knowledge then it was really not a secret anymore. Yet, it could still be labeled that way to add emphasis to its impact. If it was mainly misinformation or twisted in its retelling, there was usually no way of correcting it. If it involved major consequences, some might refrain from repeating it and then perhaps not everyone would know about it. To some extent it then remained a secret. Then, of course, there were secrets that had been made up to gain attention or for some other reason. Vows of confidentiality were good only for as long as expedient. Whatever the true nature of any secret was, to some it would be shocking while to others it might be incredulous. Some might laugh at it and others might cry. Jealousy or revenge might even be evoked. Some would dismiss it right away, and it would be forgotten. Some might be intrigued by it so as to be long remembered. There were many similarities between the law of the jungle and the law of the street.

Casey's family was typical by most appearances for the place and time, if such a thing is classifiable. His father was a furniture salesman at a wholesale outlet in Manhattan and his mother a housewife. A rarity for those days, they had intermarried. His father was Jewish and his mother Catholic. None of the neighbors much cared, although there were some trying periods with their respective families. Neither practiced any religion, and Casey was raised to believe in what his mind and heart would lead him to. Neither went to college, and his mother just finished one year of high school before she had been forced to go to work in a sweat shop in the garment district of Manhattan to help support her family. There she was a seamstress, and she worked twelve hours a day six days a week. With poor lighting and strenuous movements her eyes were ruined, and she had to wear glasses with thick lenses all of her remaining years. Her eyesight was so poor she could never drive a car. He had an older brother, Ean, six years older. They slept in the one bedroom of the apartment while his parents slept on a pullout sofa in what would have been otherwise a dining room. They ate at a table in the kitchen alcove. That sleeping arrangement was not conducive to any marital closeness, and as he deduced later in life was a major contributing factor to at least one of the dark secrets that befell the family. Relationships can be difficult when there are no impediments. They can become impossible if the obstacles are major and long lasting.

Since his father worked long hours six days a week and Casey was usually in bed by the time his father came home, he rarely saw his father and they never did develop a close relationship when he was young. It was also obvious that Ean was his favorite, and it was never easy for Casey to quite understand why a parent would have a favorite child and show no restraint in letting it be known. They did develop a closer relationship later in life, primarily because they were thrust into some dark secrets together. His father later on often expressed remorse about not being close to Casey when he was young. Ean had become such a major disappointment as well as a parental challenge.   His father would tell Casey that he turned out to be a good son and that he was proud of him.

The age difference with his brother also made it difficult for them to be close, as they could not share a real contemporary feeling. As far as Casey could tell there was a strangeness about his brother and that led to a further desire to go their separate ways. He did not know at the time that such strangeness was a tell tale sign of dark things to come, things that would deeply affect the family. Hindsight often comes too late to be useful.

Three

A couple of days arrived with warmer temperatures and the snow was nearly all melted. At this time of year, weather could change drastically. The warmer weather did not last long and it turned colder again.

The first tip Yancy had that somebody was coming was Chap barking. One of the dog's favorite pastimes was sunning himself on the front porch. Yancy looked out of the window and saw two people walking down the road. Chap was already by them, tail wagging. He grabbed his jacket and went out.

The intruders were bundled up so Yancy could not tell until he came real close to them that it was a woman and a child. The child was bent over petting Chap.

The woman was smiling as Yancy approached. "Good morning," she uttered cheerfully.

With just the face visible under a knit hat and a scarf wrapped around the neck covering close to her mouth he could not tell if she was young or old, although his guess was that she was middle aged. The child, he surmised, was a girl around ten.

"Good day," he responded. "Car break down?"

"No," the woman seemed surprised. "I am Millie's sister, and we are staying with her for awhile. Since the snow melted, we decided to take a walk. It is colder than I thought it would be."

"The weather can fool you. The road ends here."

"So I see. You must be Yancy. Millie said you are the closest neighbor."

"Yes. My dog is Chap."

"I am Sadie. My daughter is Sally."

Since it was so cold, Yancy thought about inviting them in to warm up, but he did not want to be too friendly. That might encourage further visits. "It's two miles back. Will you be able to make it? I can drive you if you want."

"Oh, we can do it. We'll just take our time."

"I like your dog, mister", Sally offered in a soft voice.

"He's real friendly. He seems to like you, too."

They started the trek back. After a few steps, Sadie turned around and shouted, "We have been gone a long time. Would you mind calling Millie and tell her we are on our way back just in case she is worried."

"Sure."

He watched them until they went around the bend in the road and were out of sight. When he returned to the house he telephoned Millie. Millie told him that Sadie had just gotten a divorce from her abusive husband in Boston and had no place to stay, so she and Sally came up here to stay with her. Sally was the real problem. She is eleven and suffers from various mental problems supposedly stemming from watching her mother being abused. Millie thought that Sally had been abused as well, although Sadie would not talk about it.

Yancy sat on the porch and thought about it all until the cold forced him back inside. He was undoubtedly not the only person who had deep dark secrets. It can make one sympathetic to know another is troubled, although it does not help with the actual bearing of one's own devil. Dark secrets can be anywhere and be harbored within anyone. As a storm within, they can consume the heart and mind.

Four

2

The children in the neighborhood went to the same high school, so the education in and out of the classroom was ongoing. On nice weather days, the long walk through the streets and by the stores on the avenue was enjoyable. Casey knew each store in detail, and was friends with all of the owners and employees. If the weather was bad, they all had student passes to take the city bus.

Children from other neighborhoods also went to the large high school. There were over 1,200 students in the freshman class. To accommodate such a mass of humanity, the school had three shifts. Freshmen went from 1-6; sophomores and juniors went from 10-3; and seniors went from 8-1. There were so many faces, so many stories, much of it was a blur as he looked back on it. Yet, puzzling as it was, there emerged two general categories of students – those that were popular and those that were not popular. The division was not based so much on appearances or accomplishments but on attitude. Those that were popular were pushy and demanding, always pretending to know how it all worked and what they were doing. They did not want to receive, opting for taking what they wanted instead. Those that were unpopular were uninformed and indifferent, almost as if they scarcely believed what was going on around them. Secrets were plentiful in the two groups as well. The popular crowd was almost proud that there were secrets. The unpopular group barely acknowledged such existed. Casey often thought he was on the dividing line between the two groups and could be with either one as he desired. The reality of it all was that he did not belong in either group and was left out of many secrets. Not that he cared that much because at that juncture of his life he did not realize the depth and power of secrets. He thought secrets more of a nuisance rather than the overwhelming burden they became later on.

Meanwhile, his brother, Ean, had gone off to college. The parents scrimped and saved for so many years for such an undertaking, yet another strain on the marriage. He was unable to adjust to such a life and drove the used car the folks had given him as a graduation present from high school to Florida. Weeks later he came home with a young buxom blonde that he professed to love. That caused quite a stir and Casey was glad he was not involved. His father gave the woman money, bought her an airline ticket back to Florida, and had a taxi take her to the airport. Many a heated discussion followed on what was to be done with Ean. He saved them an actual decision by joining the Army. For two of the following three years he was stationed in Germany and Japan. The parents still discussed his future, finally deciding they would try to get him married when he returned so that he might settle down. Casey hoped he was not the subject of any such discussions.

To avoid any further upheavals at home, Casey decided he would become a diligent student and a quiet son. That was a good all around strategy anyway. Being quiet and doing what he had to do without fuss or fanfare meant not being noticed. Some might urge that there is little benefit for being neither here nor there, but Casey was not going to argue with what seemed to work.

The high school years slid by. His exposure and experimentation with romance and friendship led him to believe he had a solid

A STORM WITHIN

foundation for later life. He preferred the school life because the home life was tense. He tried not to analyze it although he believed his mother was developing a host of mental problems. She made things uneasy for him and his father. She became more and more reclusive, and Casey had to do all of the shopping for groceries. She would not go out even for social events with her sister and brother. Her sister was a strange bird as well. His mother suffered from insomnia, so he was pretty much left on his own as she would sleep until late in the day. In those days there were few effective medicines for that condition as well as few professionals that might be able to help her generally if they could even get her to go to one.

A really sad aspect of the parental marriage was that it had, as he was told, been extra strong in the early years because they had intermarried and stood unified against society. An album of love poems in those years when his father wrote sentimental verses to his mother on special occasions revealed a special harmony. Casey never saw even the remnants of such a love. Too often he had heard of similar downfalls of strong relationships. He would experience that for himself later on.

Later in life when he looked back on his childhood, he concluded that it was a mixed bag. He was not sure he understood all he was exposed to, but it registered in his mind so that in the later years cause and effect became clearer. What settled in his heart was another story. Strong emotions cannot always be trusted. Feelings are not reliable. Fleeting feelings do not create memories. Being sorry for someone does not mean you have to do something about it. Distant memories may not always be understood. Looking back can be depressing and even dangerous.

Five

The rarely used telephone rang. Yancy hated that, knowing it was more than likely someone was going to bother him. When he picked up the receiver he glanced out of the window and noticed that it had started to snow. It was Millie and she asked him if he had seen Sally. She had packed her things in a back pack and ran away. They had gone looking for her as a blizzard was coming but had not found her. He told her that he had not seen her but would keep an eye out for her.

Just as the driving snow was thickening, there was a sound at the door. He did not hear it, although Chap did and barked accordingly. When Yancy opened the door, there was Sally covered in snow and wobbly. He pulled her gently inside and closed the door as Chap leaned in close to the little girl. Yancy brushed off the snow from her coat and wool cap as she leaned down to hug Chap. "I love your dog." The voice was weak.

"I know. He loves you, too."

Yancy telephoned Millie telling her that Sally showed up, was safe, and he would bring her back when the snow let up. Sadie got on the line. "What a relief. Thank you. She gets some wild ideas but will not be any trouble."

So, here he was alone with an eleven-year-old. He figured he would not get any writing done, and he just hoped she would be involved with Chap enough so that he would not have to do anything to entertain her.

He helped her off with the back pack and hung up her wet coat in the bathroom and put her boots in there as well. He asked her if she was hungry. She shook her head. "How about some hot chocolate?" Then came a smile and a nod of the head.

Yancy made two cups, put some marshmallows on top and they sat in chairs by the wood stove. Chap lay at Sally's feet.

"Do you have a dog at home?"

"No, and Aunt Millie does not have a dog."

"Will you be going to school?"

"I hate other children."

Not having experience with children, Yancy had no idea what would be an appropriate response to such a remark. "There are no children around here that I know of."

"They are mean," she almost shouted out.

"Not all of them."

"All of them. Grown ups, too."

"I'm a grown up."

"You have a dog."

"That makes me O.K.?"

"Yup."

"Are you tired?"

"A little."

"Why don't you lie on the sofa with Chap and take a shut eye?"

"What is a shut eye?"

"It is another way of saying a nap."

"Alright." She handed him the empty cup and went to the sofa. As she lay down Chap lay down besides her. She patted him, smiled, and the eyes closed.

Yancy checked on Sally a few times during the two hours she slept. She seemed so peaceful, and he cringed thinking that she may have suffered some physical and emotional harm by her father. Secrets can shatter the innocence of childhood. He knew that all too well. Then, as the consequences of the secrets emerge and fester over the years, the potential for life as joy is diminished and a form of perpetual drudgery takes hold so that every action and every feeling is affected. It is a curse.

Six

When Sally awoke, Yancy let Chap out the back door to do his business. The dog did not stay out long as there was a howling wind accompanying the driving snow. Yancy dried him off with a towel. "Sally, would you like to feed Chap?"

"I would like that."

"His bowl is on top of the can by the back door. Inside the can there is a scoop with his food. Fill the bowl and put it on the floor by the can. He will do the rest. You can watch as it disappears in seconds. He will devour it."

"What does devour mean?"

He liked that she was so inquisitive. "It means he will eat it fast and furious."

"Oh."

"I am making some soup for us."

"What kind?"

"Chicken."

"Does it have noodles?"

"Yes, that is the way it is right from the can."

"That will be alright, I guess. Mom makes her own chicken soup with noodles."

"I'm not much of a cook. It is just me and Chap, and you see what he eats."

"Do you get lonely?"

"Not really. I like quiet. I write books."

"Wow! I like to read."

"That's good. Reading is a good way to learn about things."

"What sort of things?"

"People, feelings, right and wrong, history, just to name a few."

Sally was pensive. "Can it help to find out why people are the way they are and why they do what they do?"

Yancy hoped he was not getting too immersed in the direction of this conversation. "It can."

"Then I want to read more. Why are kids and grown ups so mean?"

"They probably have problems of their own they are trying to overcome. They may be having trouble doing that so they lash out at whoever and whatever is nearby. It is easy to take out frustrations on someone else."

"What is a frustration?"

"It is wanting to do something and not being able to do it, or trying to do it and not succeeding at it."

Sally was quiet, and he was sure she was trying hard to digest all that he had said. "That is not how it should be."

"You are right. That is not the way it should be."

"I like the way you talk. You don't talk to me as a kid."

"You have been involved with things kids should not be involved in."

"I guess I am not really a kid anymore."

He took a moment before he responded. "Maybe, not." He wondered if she had ever had the chance to be a kid. He looked back on his own life, and he felt sorry for both of them.

Seven

3

Casey graduated from high school and faced far too many uncertainties for a youngster. He would have preferred to go to college over working at some menial job, but he had no idea what he wanted to study and had not even a glimmer of interest in any profession. He was not alone. It seems as if every generation is a lost generation with respect to the where, what, and when the crossing over into adulthood might occur. It takes a special vision for an eighteen-year-old to grasp when a foothold in the future will appear. Sometimes, it takes long preparation and an extended period of apprehension. Sometimes, it just happens. Apparently, for some it never happens.

He thought about joining the Peace Corp., but the thought of going off to some strange foreign land loomed too large and intimidating. So, the decision of least resistance was to enroll in Brooklyn College in a Liberal Arts program and await a dawning. Preparing for nothing special seemed right up his alley.

Ean left the Army, and he was introduced and coerced into dating a young woman, Carol, also floundering and whose parents were anxious to marry her off. It was no match made in Heaven but perhaps the stars were aligned for the moment. To get their respective parents off their backs the two agreed to get married. Both families *were prepared to do whatever it took to sustain them, and it was awhile before Ean found a suitable job as a draftsman's apprentice. The job was in Chicago, which made it even better, as the couple moved away from being daily reminders of parental failure. The couple also thought they would fare better being away from the overbearing parents. They say blood is thicker than water, but cold blood brings elements of its own, and not necessarily good ones. Two sons were born, first Ned and two years later, Eldrich. After Ean became a full draftsman they moved to California to take advantage of a good job offer and to further distance themselves from the families. The sad part was that the couple did not really love each other and the future was bleak. In fact, it was doomed.*

In the meantime, Casey graduated from Brooklyn College and then went to Brooklyn Law School after he discovered a certain fascination in the law. He passed the bar and became an associate in a Manhattan mega law firm. He became engaged to a woman he met at a firm party and he was told the woman came from a wealthy family and would be an asset for his career. The marriage did not last long as Casey did not actually know or appreciate what love and emotional commitments were. He was not sure he ever would.

Not hearing from Ean over all of those years, Ean did call him once he learned that Casey had become a lawyer. He asked him to do him a favor. When still in Chicago Ean had gotten arrested and fined for public indecency, the details of the act made Casey cringe. He wanted Casey to get that criminal record expunged. Casey was able to do that, and never even received a thank you. Little did he know at the time that their next conversation would be at his initiation.

Ean and Carol finally divorced as the effort to sustain the marriage was too great. It proved to be hard on the boys, very hard. When teenagers, Ned ran away to join a religious cult and Eldrich committed suicide. Being a very sensitive boy, he was badly bullied at school and was unable to receive offsetting solace from a shaken home. The effect on Ean was devastating. He could not concentrate on work and was fired, and he was unable to function constructively. His guilt percipitated a downward spiral of his life. Casey flew out to California to console him and to try and fortify his thinking and get him on a right track, but it was useless. The only thing he wound up doing was to give him money, and that was the start of an unending support that he did not want to do but felt he had no other alternative. Ean's desperateness for money became a road to disaster.

Their father also sent money secretly to Ean whenever he could as their mother would not approve of such a thing and wanted nothing to do with Ean. Her mental deterioration was in full swing. The father, in an attempt to try something drastic to change things moved them to a condo in a retirement village in Florida. Casey called them once a week in a futile effort to keep a family image alive. His mother would repeat a host of complaints about his father, Florida, and the world in general. Each call was depressing. His father would call him regularly secretly to keep him informed on his mother's mental and emotional fragmentation and to also unburden himself as he had nobody to talk to and it did help him that Casey knew what was going on and how miserable he was. They became close that way. Casey was part of a family nightmare all around and it eroded his spirit. His own pursuit of any happiness was put on hold, and it tore at his heart how miserable his father was having to live with his mother and the failure he felt with Ean. The family life in its entirety as well as each of its component parts was a nightmare and a seething deep dark secret. Of course, he had no way of knowing at the time that the worst was yet to come.

Eight

When Yancy finished his writing for the day, he checked on Sally. She was sitting on the sofa with Chap watching a show on the television. She glanced at him and smiled all the while patting Chap who was in his glory. The blizzard was still raging outside, the snow piling up. He brought in some more wood from the pile under the tarp on the back porch and put it in the stove. "How about spaghetti for supper?"

"I love sgetties," Sally shouted out with animation.

"Hey, me as well. It's actually my favorite, and easy to make. Pasta comes in a box and the sauce in a jar."

"Make a lot. I am really hungry. My mom makes her own sauce. She is a good cook and likes to cook."

"Sure enough. You are still growing."

They ate at the small table in the kitchen. Sally grinned when she saw her plate piled high. "Looks good to me."

"I hope so. I don't have any milk. Water will have to do."

"That's alright."

Sally could not finish it all. She ate more than he thought she would since she was just a little thing. "I think I pigged out," she said with a big sigh.

"You did good."

"Sure was good."

"Glad you liked it. I have some doughnuts in the freezer. I can microwave one for you for dessert."

"I have had enough."

"I will give it to you for breakfast with some eggs."

"That will be good, but I am so full now I can't think about eating."

He laughed. He sure did like this little girl. He was not sure when children develop a distinct personality, but Sally had reached that plateau despite, or maybe because of, any horror in her life.

Sadie telephoned and thanked him for taking care of Sally. She then talked to her daughter for awhile. The little girl rattled off all that had happened, and particularly raved about Chap, the chicken soup and the sgetties.

Sally could barely keep her eyes open. Her trek through the snow had been exhausting and the nap had not been nearly enough to fully revitalize her. He made a bed for her on the sofa and moved Chap's bed from the bedroom to besides the sofa.

The snow fell heavily all night but had tapered off by morning. When Yancy woke up it was just flurrying outside. Sally was still fast asleep as he made some coffee after letting Chap out. He was drinking his second cup at the table when Sally woke up after Chap licked her face.

As promised, he made her scrambled eggs with the doughnut, and she ate with gusto. "You sure are taking good care of me. Mom would be happy."

"I have had little contact with children."

"How come you don't have children?"

"I was not married long enough to have any."

"Oh."

"After you digest breakfast, you can go out with Chap because he likes to play in the snow. Maybe, you can make a snowman."

"O.K."

The snow was too deep for the little girl, and it was even difficult for Chap to romp around in. They were not outside for very long. All of Sally's clothes were wet, and after she changed he hung them up in the bathroom.

Later, just as Yancy was about to go to the kitchen to make some lunch, there was a banging on the door. Chap barked loudly. It was Sadie, completely snow covered. "It took me two hours to get here, but I made it. I did not want Sally to be a burden to you. We can make it back as soon as I rest for awhile."

He ushered her in and helped her out of her coat. He could tell she was tired. Walking through deep snow is not easy. Without a coat and hat, she was a pleasant looking person, although a bit plump. He guessed her to be in her late thirties, and the short red hair looked real. "We were about to have lunch. Rest while I get some sandwiches together. Sally is no burden, and I think you should wait until the snow clears a bit and I can drive you back."

She must have realized just how tired she was. "I don't want to be an imposition."

"We'll make the best of it. Sally has been no trouble, really. In fact, I have enjoyed her company."

"We'll try not to bother you. Can I use your phone to call Millie and let her know what is going on?"

"Sure. I will get some lunch together, and then you might want to crash."

While working in the kitchen he could hear Sadie and Sally talking. Sally was telling her that Yancy was an author and that the books he had written were lined up on the book shelf.

There was pleasant casual conversation during lunch, and for what she had been through Yancy thought Sadie seemed to be relaxed and talkative. She may have been tense at first because of the present anxiety over Sally, but she was reassured that Yancy was no threat.

Just as they were finishing, it started to snow again. "I don't think you are going anywhere today," Yancy announced.

"I am sorry," Sadie offered. "The last thing I intended was to make things more difficult for you."

"Not a problem. There are two bedrooms, although only one bed. I use the other bedroom as my writing space. You and Sally can sleep tonight in the bed and I will camp out on the sofa. Chap will probably want to be there with Sally. Hopefully, the weather will be much better tomorrow."

Yancy retreated to do some writing while Sadie and Sally along with Chap sat on the sofa. He figured Sadie would doze off as soon as he was out of sight. It did not feel as much of an infringement on his privacy as he thought it might be. Chap certainly was enjoying all of the attention. Yancy actually felt comfortable with their presence. Perhaps, there was some sort of social need in him after all.

Nine

Yancy did not get much writing done. His mind wandered, and a self debate is not conducive to creative endeavors. An examination of who he was today and what a future might be like was probably an analysis long overdue, and he found himself mentally and emotionally thrust into it. To a large extent he was satisfied with his writing, and he was especially pleased that he had now transposed himself as Casey to give expression to the haunting family secrets that had caused so much anguish in his life. The question arose that because of this had he purposely deprived himself of certain meaningful facets of life so that in his old age he had nothing to show for his living except his books? Was the entry into his life by Sadie and Sally a way to rectify that? Was it an opportunity to capture what he never had? Was it a chance to do some good for others at the same time? Was he entitled to, and would he know how to handle, some final rewards?

When Yancy came back to the main area of the house, Sally was watching television with Chap fast asleep sprawled across her lap. Sadie was sitting in the arm chair by the window reading one of his books. The snow was still falling. "Things that boring here that you have to resort to reading one of my books?"

"You write very well, although I need a dictionary for some of the words you use. I used to read a lot, but have gotten away from it over the years. I realize I miss it. Books are a magical world."

"That they are. In a book one can find a lifetime of experiences and thoughts, as well as dreams and hopes. A choice of words can be arbitrary but I try to capture the word which is best for the essence of what and where it is in the story or what and where my mood is at the moment."

"I can relate to that. When I was in college, I had an English professor who said something similar. Words are a source of the magic."

"What did you major in?"

"Journalism."

"Did you work in the field?"

"For awhile."

"Millie told me why you are staying with her. I am sorry you had to go through that."

"Millie talks too much, and says things which should not be said. It was a bad experience, and even worse for Sally."

"How long are you going to stay?"

Sadie did not answer right away. "I don't know. I am not in a position to make plans just yet. She has said I can stay as long as I want to, but it is not a comfortable situation." She stared at the snow out of the window as if it might reinforce her thinking. "I don't know why I am telling you all of this. It's my problem."

"I am glad you have. I have an idea that you might want to think about. I am an old man. I have let certain aspects of life pass me by for reasons best left unsaid. I have now become a hermit by necessity rather than by choice. I have always wondered what I may have missed by not having children. I have gotten a taste of it by having Sally here. She is a delight. I think she would be good for me, and I could be a steadying influence on her, grandfather style. A glimpse into a world where not all men are bad. She is already attached to Chap. You both would be welcome here for as long as you wish to stay. The house is small and I use the second bedroom as my writing area, but I can write anywhere and it can be converted to a living space for the two of you. Peace and calm will make healing a possibility."

Sadie did not answer right away. "It is very kind and generous of you. It is something I need to think about for awhile. I am not sure you realize you might get more than you contemplate. Your life would no longer be your own. That might be too big an adjustment. Sally and I are both emotionally beaten up and the fragility promises to be around for a long time. I suspect healing will be anything but tranquil."

"I am willing to try it."

"I am not sure what is best for us at this point. Frankly, I am not sure about anything."

"Enough said. It is entirely up to you. I have said my piece. How about I make us some supper?"

"Let me make it. I already have looked around at what you have, and I believe I can put something together."

He smiled. "Do your thing. Of course, I have only stocked up for one so you might be duly challenged."

"I like challenges."

Sally was right. Her mother was a good cook, particularly since she really did not have that much to work with. It was the best meal he had in a long time.

Ten

Sadie and Sally slept in the bed while Yancy bedded down on the sofa. It was no problem for him. When he was young he had trouble sleeping unless he was in his own bed. As an old man, he could sleep anywhere, anytime. He wondered why that was so, and mentally he added it to the list of the things in life he experienced and yet were unexplained. The list kept getting longer, and he suspected that few items would ever get removed.

It had stopped snowing. It would still be another day before he could take them back if it did not snow anymore.

Sadie and Sally built a snowman and Chap romped around nearby. He could hear their laughter from the house, and it was a truly wonderful sound. Even if just for the moment, it can overtake the misery brooding within.

Sadie made lunch, and then later she prepared supper. They talked most of the afternoon and evening. He found her to be well informed, a good listener, and evidently enjoyed intellectual banter. She had finished his book and was anxious to talk about it, and expressed a desire to read all of his other works. He hesitated when she asked him about the book he was working on now. He offered just a general comment as it was far too serious for him to elaborate about it just yet. If he told her it was about dark secrets emerging from the shadows it might be too relevant to her own life. Dark living very easily becomes dark secrets. It is too bad that the one life a person has can be consumed by such happenings. He knew that better than most other people, and he had the feeling that Sadie was learning that as well. His motive for writing the new book was not to depress others, although it might easily be interpreted that way. In one of his earlier books he had thought he had elaborated on a situation and its consequences sufficiently so that readers would conclude as he intended, only to find out that some completely missed the point and derived a different outcome. He blamed himself for that.

The next day, the weather had cleared and the temperature rose so he was able to drive them back to Millie's house. Sally gave Chap a big hug, and then she turned and gave Yancy one as well. Sadie seemed more relaxed. She thanked him again and reiterated that she would think about his kind offer.

Once back, he noted how quiet it was in the house as Chap kept looking for Sally. He felt something he had rarely felt before – a kind of loneliness. He thought that such had a special meaning for him at this juncture, and he hoped that Sadie would decide to move over. It was not that he needed other people, although the two represented a human association he had separated himself from. Sadie was someone to talk to, to share thoughts. Sally was a youthful presence of curiosity and bewilderment that he knew existed but had not been close to. If it did come to pass, it might be that they would wind up doing more for him than he was going to do for them. Mutual reliance is a strong foundation for relationships.

The desire to get back to writing took hold, and the need to vent his history and its interpretation led him to the writing space where he was alone with his thoughts. That, too, was a form of loneliness, albeit a self-imposed one.

A STORM WITHIN

Eleven

4

His father's telephone calls became more frantic as the situation with his mother worsened and became more desperate. Casey felt badly that his father had to endure such a situation as his mother would never agree to seek psychiatric help for as far as she was concerned her husband and the rest of the world was the problem. He visited them one weekend a month and stayed with his mother while his father could have a respite.

Ean's downward spiral exacerbated the situation. Ean was a basket case, riddled with guilt and he lashed out at the world. He would not work, and Casey and his father kept sending him money just to keep him going. The mother knew nothing of all of this and blamed her husband for Ean's distancing him from the family.

His mother developed an advanced stage of stomach cancer, and the pain medication further contributed to her outlandish behavior and demands. The medicine also led to her sleeping for long periods, a small blessing. At one point the doctor admitted her to the hospital for further tests. Casey went to Florida to give comfort to both parents.

His father pleaded with him to talk as a lawyer to the doctor to hasten death so that he could finally be set free from his torment. Casey was reluctant to do that, but his father pressed the issue. Finally, he agreed. At first, the doctor would not go along with it as it was unlawful to do so. Casey used all of his best lawyer skills to forcefully argue that this situation required such drastic action, the most persuasive reasoning involving the effect on his father of his mother's mental state. The doctor finally agreed to administer extra morphine and swore Casey and his father to secrecy.

For awhile Casey was able to convince himself that considering all of the factors he had done the right thing. Gradually, his thinking was swayed differently. He could not escape the fact that he had in effect killed his mother. Hastening a death, even if determined to be eventual, is not a strong reason to perform such a harsh act. Perhaps, she might have recovered. Freeing his father from mental and emotional bondage was not an adequate reason to justify shortening his mother's life. The same assertive effort might have been made to bring psychiatric assistance to the situation. The unknowns of the future only become a reality when there is a future.

Over the years, he relived that situation many times. It ate at his moral core, and he found himself suffering from great remorse. It crept into his soul and nestled there obliterating most attempts to find normalcy in his own life. A situation that cannot be relived or adequately compensated for becomes an increasing burden. It intensifies and perpetuates the storm within. He really had no right to convince another to break the law and to violate his professional oath. Perhaps, if this had been the only deep dark secret Casey might still have eventually found some peace. However, another event bringing on such an effect was to come, and there was no way for Casey to know that it would be deeper and darker.

Twelve

Two days later Sadie telephoned. "Kind sir, do you still want us?"

"Surely," the response was genuine and emphatic.

"Then we will be over later, baggage and all. I told Millie you wanted to hire me as a housekeeper, so I might as well make some money while here. Millie is alright with that since I will still be close by. George is relieved, I know."

"I really don't have money to pay you a salary."

"Oh, that is not really expected. It just made it easier for the telling of it."

"Understood."

"Thank you, again."

"I should be thanking you."

"You may wind up changing your mind."

"I doubt it. Tomorrow we will go to town to get you beds and a dresser. You can decide whether you want twin beds or the two of you can sleep in a larger one. The room can hold it either way, I am sure. The furniture store will deliver them. We'll need to get pillows, sheets, and towels as well. I have enough blankets. Then, we can stock up at the food store."

"See, we are trouble already."

"That's not trouble. It is entertainment."

She laughed. The first laugh since the time she and Sally made the snowman. There had not been many opportunities to laugh, and as such each brought on a special meaning. Hope brings its own chance of an expectancy fulfilled.

When he hung up the telephone he was further surprised at himself for going along with this plan so easily. Usually so wary and reserved with people, he was opening up more to have them come live with him. It was probably the early alone time that he had with Sally that chipped away at his reserve. It took a child to melt his heart.

The book he was working on, Dark Secrets, was a depressing tome, a great variance from the uplifting books he had already written. Writing about the secrets was a form of reliving them, and it added greater fury to the raging storm within. Even though it was his way of unburdening himself, he wondered if it was the best thing to do now. Perhaps, this one he would not seek to get published and merely keep it as a sort of diary of his true being. After all, just the writing was his catharsis, the way of shedding light on a dark past. Piercing the depths with words set on paper might be sufficient to satisfy his need to reveal submerged truths. There was time to make any such decision since the book was far from finished, and he knew there would be much to debate with himself about it. The nature of the book might change with this new house arrangement. For a man whose life had been run heretofore on close to a fixed agenda, he was now going to be exposed to a series of potential unknowns. The largest unknown might be a reevaluation of who he was and what he was to do with whatever time he had left in this life.

Thirteen

Chap alerted Yancy to their arrival. Sadie's car pulled up in the driveway next to the carport where he kept his car. As soon as he opened the front door, Chap bolted out to greet them. When Yancy reached the car to help them with the baggage, Sally stood up after hugging Chap to hug him. He was pleased by such a spontaneous action. He was even more pleased when Sadie also hugged him. There is no denying that an old man appreciates a hug from young and younger, and it was a form of reaffirmation that he was doing the right thing by having them with him.

Until a dresser would come, not much could be unpacked. Some of the loose clothing and coats on hangers went right into the closet. There was also a bag of laundry. Yancy showed Sadie how to operate the washing machine and dryer in the laundry room.

"Feels like home already," Sadie said as she sat down in a chair. "Let me rest a spell and then I will make supper."

"Fine, whenever. You will find that the true beauty of this home is that there are no demands, no schedules, no expectancies. You do whatever and whenever your spirit moves you."

"I like the sound of that, and appreciate it more than you know. It just may take me some time to get used to it."

"Time stands still, well almost still, on a country road."

"Maybe, I should have looked for a country road early on. Maybe, I should have done a bunch of things early on that I had no idea were out there."

"As long as you are breathing, it is never too late for anything."

"One of the first things I am going to do is to finish reading all of your books. There must be great wisdom in them."

"I don't know about that. It is actually more that when one gets old one can look back and see that there were more choices than might have been apparent at the time, and some things are not set in cement and can be changed with will and opportunity."

"Sometimes it is really too late."

"Yes, sometimes. But, as you may find out, I hope, things can be made better because of lessons learned and dreams elevated."

"I do hope so, for Sally's sake."

"For you as well."

"It all sounds well and good, but I think I have a long way to go. One thing I have learned well, and have no reasonable explanation for, is that a good experience disappears in an instant while a bad experience lingers, and often with great pain."

"I am hoping that by being here such a bad experience will have led you to a better place and with a brighter future for you both."

She smiled at his kind remarks, but at the moment she had little faith in dreams.

Fourteen

It took a good part of the day to pick out and arrange for delivery of twin beds and a dresser, to buy sheets and pillowcases, and then to do a food shopping with extra provisions in the event the winter was bad. As a treat, they had lunch at the one diner in the town, and Sally especially enjoyed a milkshake with a hamburger and fries.

"I feel bad you could not get to write today," Sadie commented on the drive back to the house.

"No need to feel that way. It was a nice break. I don't write by a schedule. I don't write every day, and at times maybe only a paragraph or so. Writing requires much meditation, and for an old writer it takes time and energy for the imagination to get cranked up, if at all. It is not anything I can force or deny. When all the forces come together I write. If they are not congealed, I languish in the world of writing pretension. One author's secret, especially an old author, if an idea comes to mind at a random moment, I make a hand written note of it. There is always the chance the wind will carry it away or the dust will cover it up. Other secrets abound."

This was not the time for an in-depth conversation on secrets. Sadie did not pick up on the remark anyway. "Tomorrow, you can write if the forces cooperate. I will be taking Sally to the County Education Department Building. I need to enroll her in a home school program and pick up all the necessary materials. I would prefer she went to school because I think the social interaction would be good for her, but she is so fragile right now that it would not take much to upset her."

"I'll be glad to help with the schooling."

"Nice of you to offer. We'll see if I can even handle it. I am not sure what is involved."

"And, what are we going to do to get you back to a sure place?"

"I'm a big girl in case you haven't noticed. I bruise easily, and it may be a long climb up, but I will make it. I am sure it will take time, although thanks to you not as long as it would otherwise."

"That's the right attitude. I think human progress is mainly attitude. I am not a whole person as you have probably guessed from the way I live, but since I have started my new book, as well as having the two of you as my guests, my attitude has improved greatly."

"I would be happy to do for you what you are doing for us."

"I think that will happen on its own just as a fallout from everything else. I fool myself into thinking that I live as a hermit by choice, but over the years it has turned into a necessity."

"I am not sure I understand what you are saying."

"I do not mean to be talking in riddles. I am sure we will have many conversations where my life will become clearer to you as well as yours to me. The great benefit will be if we can both see it clearer for ourselves as well."

She did not respond, although he was sure she was thinking about what he had just said. He glanced sideways and decided she had a friendly face to match her disposition. It was easy to talk with her, and he had the sense that she would not judge him or his life just as he would not draw unnecessary conclusions about her and her life. An open and receptive relationship would be good for both of them. It certainly would provide a positive atmosphere for Sally.

Fifteen

5

The situation with Ean was indeed unfortunate for everyone. His behavior, if Casey had to describe it, was bizarre. Casey should have objected to his increasing demands for money, although it was obvious from his mental and economic condition that it was all that was keeping him going. There was no satisfaction in knowing that by repeatedly sending him money all that Casey was achieving was perpetuating the feeding of a limitless desperation. There was no appreciation by Ean.

Casey should have been wary each and every time that Ean brought up the subject of their father's eventual death. He urged repeatedly to have the unit in the retirement village sold and all the proceeds sent to him as Casey did not need any of the money while he did. He said that Casey would then be relieved from sending him any of his own money. Casey reluctantly agreed, and in hindsight that would have been the time to agree to it only on the terms that such proceeds be sent in installments rather than in a lump sum. Ean would undoubtedly go through the money rather quickly and Casey would be thrust back into the role of a provider.

Casey should also have been suspicious when Ean asked him to buy for him a round trip airline ticket to Florida so he might visit their father for a week. Even though he had not expressed such a desire before, he said he wanted to be with him for awhile. Casey thought it would be good for the father, so he agreed to it.

It was on the third night of that visit that Ean telephoned Casey to tell him that their father had died. He had fallen in the bathroom and had hit his head on the sink. As with any death, the police were called and looked into it before the body was taken to the crematorium as Casey had arranged some time ago.

Ean was back in California less than a week when he telephoned Casey to find out if the sale had been arranged. It was soon thereafter and a low offer was accepted as the real estate market in Florida was depressed at the time. The funds were sent to Ean from the closing.

Over the years, the thought that the death was not truly an accident grew in Casey's mind and became more troubling in his outlook. Eventually, he had to face a stark truth and admit to himself that he believed Ean had murdered their father. The police investigation was merely routine and they had been led to believe that an old man merely had an accident. That thought further ate at his soul, and there were few calm moments after that.

As feared, the money did not last long for Ean's existence. Casey had to resume sending him money. It further unnerved him that he was enabling a murderer.

Two years later, Ean died from a sudden heart attack. Ned telephoned him with the news, and he admitted that he had long ago become disenchanted with Ean. He had not only considered him to be a bad father but he also blamed him for Eldrich's death.

Casey was the only one who knew the full and true story. He had caused the premature death of his mother, and his brother had murdered their father. He was immersed in a deep dark secret where sunlight cannot reach and the heart is encased in ice. Most people need to live through and overcome disappointments and failures. Not *many, as Casey viewed it, had to endure knowing that their soul is an abyss. Lives had been altered, bent to accommodate evil desires. There is no way to redeem the soul from this. There is no way to remedy what had been done. There is no way to go on in anything that approaches a normal life. Casey was a broken man. It was a living death.*

Sixteen

Yancy had always enjoyed the first morning cup of hot coffee, especially in cold weather. This morning was no different as he sat sipping the coffee at the kitchen table.

Sally, still in pajamas and rubbing the sleep from her eyes, came into the kitchen. She bent down to hug Chap who had already been up, out, and fed. "Mom is still asleep."

"Looks like you are still asleep, too."

"I was looking for Chap. He wasn't in his bed."

"He came out when he heard me, and he had to go out."

"Do you want me to feed him?"

"Later. He has already had his breakfast. Speaking about eating, would you like some cold cereal while there is still a supply of milk?"

"Sure. When Mom gets up I start school today."

"That will be fun."

"Can Chap stay with me at school?"

"He will probably want to be with you."

"I love him."

"I know, and he knows. He loves you back."

"I love you. Do you love me back?"

"For sure." He hugged her and she was all smiles.

He watched her as she ate the cereal. He did love her, and in a way he was surprised how easy it was to love. It, again, made him think what it might have been like if he had children of his own. Was it easy to love her because she was a child? After all of the long periods of his life where he struggled with secrets and his inability to give completely of himself, was it now that he was ready to love? Or, was the writing revelation of the deep dark secrets freeing his soul to feel the kind of emotions that were difficult to hold on to earlier? Was his heart now open?

"Why do you live by yourself?"

"I am not by myself. Chap is here. I used to live in the city but it was not conducive to writing."

"What is conducive?"

"It was not easy to write. Too many distractions."

"What are distractions?"

"Things that don't let you concentrate on what you are doing."

"Do you get lonely?"

"Sometimes, but not with you here."

"Do you have children?"

"No. I wish I did though, especially a little girl like you."

"Were you ever married?"

"When I was much younger. It did not last."

"Why?"

Just then Sadie came into the kitchen, tightening the belt on her robe. "Lots of talking going on here."

"One little girl asks a whole bunch of questions. There is coffee in the pot. Sally has already had cereal."

"It was good," Sally chimed in. "Mr. Yancy could be a teacher. He knows about everything."

"Everything is awfully big, even for me." He was emphatic.

Sadie smiled as she took the first sip of coffee from the cup. "I think you are going to be constantly tested on everything you do know."

"I suspect you are right. I better reread the Book of Everything."

"Can I read it?" Sally nearly shouted it out.

"As soon as I finish writing it."

Seventeen

Yancy had cleared out a corner of his bedroom to do his writing, although he did not feel much like writing this day. He could hear Sadie and Sally working on the school lessons in the living room, and that was not so much a distraction as the gloom that hung over his fictional character, Casey. For emphasis on the theme of the book, Casey was inconsolable. His life would never be totally his own as long as the haunting secrets festered in his soul. But, was it the same for Yancy? Much of his life had been negatively impacted by such, and it was a contributing factor to a host of unhappy times and events. It was undoubtedly a primary cause of his personality shortcomings. Yet, there was sufficient mental and emotional fortitude to not let it rule his entire life. The arrival of Sadie and Sally brought that to the forefront. He had planned to expand on Casey as a broken man because of the deep dark secrets he harbored within his being and that such can be an all consuming burden, a never ending storm within. Now, he had to consider whether there could be offsetting factors and influences to lessen that kind of impact. Might, for example, the love of a child as a day-to-day constant overshadow the harsh reality of dealing with large consuming negatives? For the book, now that he had revealed the essence of those deep dark secrets could he adequately treat in believable fashion the entry into Casey's life of a person to mend his being, even in part? Would or could he adapt that to his own life? Little wonder an unknown barely taking form in his agitated mind prevented him from writing.

At the end of the day, life is the greatest unknown. A person can trudge through most of it in the shadow of his own making. At any given moment sunlight might pierce that darkness bringing forth new vistas, new opportunities to venture out into what had previously been a hostile self world. It might be a sudden changing or a gradual transition, and some might be apprehensive about it and slip back into the shadow or merely turn away from it so that it need not be considered. For Yancy, he was perceptive enough to recognize that the sunlight was a little girl. He wanted to embrace it completely but was not sure where it might take him. Perhaps, it was too late for him. Maybe he was too old to absorb new feelings and to attempt to navigate around in uncharted waters. In spite of that, he was eager to find out.

Eighteen

That evening after Sally went to sleep, Sadie pulled another one of Yancy's books from the shelf and started to read it. She seemed relaxed, and he was pleased she wanted to read his writings.

"After you have gone through the whole bunch, I would like you to read what I have done so far in the new book. It is completely different from the earlier works. In those I have tried to emphasize and apply the lessons of life for the purposes of having and pursuing dreams. In this one there is no opportunity for dreaming and all aspects of a positive life are overshadowed by a series of life events."

"Is there a reason for the change?"

"Yes, but I don't want to depress you."

"Believe me, I cannot be more depressed than I already am. Only two things keep me going – Sally and my medications. When I was young, I believed I could build a life I wanted. I have since learned that once whatever you have is destroyed it is not only more difficult to rebuild a life but it is also impossible to tell what may be salvaged and what any rebuilt life might be like."

"I believe you can make it whatever you want it to be. You need to give yourself time to weigh the options."

"If only that were so. I made a real poor choice for a husband, maybe because I was too anxious to be married and have a family. It ruined my life and soured my daughter on people and things."

"A dog is turning your daughter away from her past, and you

will find the key to happiness as well. If you do not believe that, it will probably never happen."

"You are as uplifting as your books."

"They are purposely that way. Darkness in my own life compels me to show others that there can be light. I am hoping you will see that for yourself."

"I am afraid I have a long way to go."

"Each journey starts with the first step."

"So, why the change now?"

"I'll leave the details until later when you get to that read, but old age compels me to revisit my life not only to clear away the cobwebs of a tenuous memory but also to validate my death."

"As Sally would say, I don't really understand that."

"Understanding comes with the particulars. You may be able to piece them together as I have done to take a form of action concerning them."

"You certainly are a man of mystery."

"The title of the book is Dark Secrets. The secrets are the mystery and not the man."

"You already know my secrets without the details."

He did not respond right away. "A tragic life is not a secret. It is a regret."

Nineteen

Millie invited them for the Thanksgiving meal. Yancy gave an excuse for not attending and explained to Sadie his aversion for social activities. Sadie and Sally went, and Sadie left extra portions of the side dishes she had made for the feast so that Yancy could have them in their absence.

That absence gave him a dual opportunity. It reinforced a feeling of loneliness without them there, a feeling not often experienced and its significance was duly registered in his mind and heart. It also gave him a further chance to dwell upon what Casey's future might be as well as the road ahead for himself.

Chap kept looking out the window for Sally's return as Yancy sat by the wood stove munching on the food Sadie left for him. His mind wandered in many directions. The major problem with recollections is that not all the details may be remembered. So, it is the remembered details which form the impression and dictate its significance. If it is still not a clear picture, a guess at some of the details may have to be made, a guess which may not be accurate. Therefore, the memory of what happened may not be truly reflective of the actual event. That was not the case with the family secrets since those events are relived so frequently that nearly all of the details are intact. The emotional trauma reinforces a degree of clarity. Other incidents, however, even as related to such secrets, may be fuzzy and their significance only acknowledged by their relation to other events or persons involved.

His childhood then was not necessarily completely as he had lived it. Then, the same would also be true for Casey. His past was his past even though it was also his own past. Would that also be true for his future and what was ahead for Casey? What he might see for himself with a positive influence by Sadie and Sally did not mean it should be that way for Casey. To emphasize the consequences of the deep dark secrets, there probably should be no hint of happiness for Casey. Yet, the book was depressing enough in describing Casey's past. Should a reader of the book be rewarded for trudging through the blackness by a glimmer of light as by a beacon from a lighthouse to reveal that all life can take a turn for the better? Can even the darkest of secrets be borne because a degree of ascent from the depths is possible? If the reader deserves that slight breath of relief, should the author effectuate it? Or, should a dark story remain in the abyss so that its purpose is fully acknowledged? Would or should a strike of the pen alter the story's impact and personal design? Yancy's dilemma for Casey, reflective to a degree of his own, was could what lay ahead be more important than what lay behind? In the final analysis he was the master of Casey's future as well as his own.

Twenty

An early morning alone time for Yancy and Sally became an enjoyable routine. Even when the milk was gone until the next shopping trip if feasible, Yancy would make some sort of breakfast for her to have while he drank his coffee.

"Mr. Yancy, do you like having me here?"

"I sure enough do."

"Do you know why I ask that?"

"No."

"Nobody has ever told me they like having me."

"I am sure your mother has told you."

"She doesn't count. She is my mother."

"Well, I really like having you here. You know Chap feels the same way."

"I like being here."

"I'm glad."

"No yelling and no hitting."

"There won't be any of that here ever."

"Can I stay here forever?"

"As long as you and your mother want to."

"How long is forever?"

"Forever means different things to different people. It is what can be called a fuzzy word. It can be as long as needed or wanted."

"I don't understand that."

"I am not sure I fully understand it myself. Some things are meant to be even if we do not fully understand them."

"I don't understand that either."

"When you are older I think you will."

"Why are there some things I can't understand until I am older?"

He sure did appreciate her probing curiosity. "Because it takes experience to see it clearly. It is also a reason to want to get older."

"What kind of experience?"

"Doing all sorts of things, meeting many different people."

"I hate people."

"I know, but that won't always be true."

"It will be for mean people."

"Most people are not mean. In fact, many people are kind and friendly."

"Not fathers or children."

"Yes, many fathers and especially many children. You will have a whole bunch of friends some day who will love you and you will love them."

"It will be forever until then."

"I hope not."

Twenty-One

6

A haunting past is not in the past. It is in the present and, more than likely, in the future as well. Casey tried to keep it all in perspective, and he found that burying himself in his work helped to subdue some of his anxiety. However, it surfaced in his mind and heart often. His sleep was restless, and eating was merely a habit and not an enjoyable venture. He distanced himself from the few friends he had, and when not working he wallowed in self guilt. The repercussions of what we do may be huge and long-lasting.

It had been over a year since the law firm encouraged its members to volunteer for community outreach programs. Casey had selected to sign up for SUDAD, the Surrogate Dad Program. He had forgotten all about that commitment until he received the notice at his office that an assignment had been made for him. He was to meet with Emilee Rodriquez, a Latino freshman with no father at The School for Performing Arts, on Tuesdays at 1:30 for a half hour in Room 103 at the school during study period. He had no idea what to expect, and was actually not prepared or wanting to do it since his mind was preoccupied with so many other matters. There was really no way he could sidestep this undertaking.

Casey figured Emilee was probably thirteen and had to be

artistically talented to have gained entrance to that school. Since his experience with and knowledge about children was nil, other than what he might know from his own unusual childhood, he had no idea what he should or could say to her. There was no information supplied by the program administration except to be friendly and a good listener. She probably felt the same way.

Emilee may have been thirteen but she looked much younger. Being short and extremely thin were not teenager features. Unruly long black hair with bangs over piercing black eyes and a thin elongated face with pinched lips were what he noticed first. The black eyes checked him out.

They were alone in the room after the teacher introduced them and left. He thought he better say something first. "You can call me Casey. What shall I call you?"

There was no smile, and she did not respond right away. "Call me whatever you like." The voice was too harsh for a small body. "This is not my idea."

"Mine, neither. Let's just make the best of it."

"I like to be called Lee."

"Alright, Lee. I am here because you don't have a father. I am not married and have no children. In fact, I don't even know any children to talk to and this will be a first for me as well. Maybe, this will be a win-win situation."

"I doubt it"

"Of course, I was a child once myself, but there are far too many things about being a child that I do not remember. Memory fades as we get older." Not even a smile from her. "I have very real-like dreams now, so real they often wake me up. I can't remember if I dreamed at all when I was a boy. Do you dream?"

The black eyes widened, and Casey had the impression she was really looking at him for the first time. "I do, I guess, but I don't remember them. What do you dream about that it wakes you up?"

"I suppose they are rightly nightmares. They involve me in situations that are scarey or frustrating, and as hard as I may try there is no way I can help myself. I have even dreamed of dying."

He could tell he had aroused her interest. "Why do you think you have bad dreams?"

"I know why I have bad dreams. There are dark secrets in my past, and dark secrets are powerful stuff."

"What are dark secrets?"

"Happenings that were very sad or very disappointing, and people who were not who they should have been."

"I don't understand all that."

"If it happens, you will then know."

"I should know then. My father, from the little I remember because I was really young, would beat my mother and me for no reason, especially when he was drunk."

"Where is he now?"

"Who knows and who cares? Mom says he just disappeared one day and has not been heard from since. Good riddance, I say."

"That is a dark secret."

"Mom has struggled ever since. She does not smile and never laughs. She works the late shift at an all-night diner. She loves me I am sure, but she never hugs or kisses me. When she talks to me she doesn't look me in the eyes like you are doing now. What do you think that means?"

"It probably means she feels badly for you and for herself."

"How can you tell if somebody feels badly?"

"As with your mother, they avoid close contact and cut conversations short. They try to cover it up so nobody will notice. Actually, what they are doing is making it more obvious."

"Do adults feel badly the way they treat children?"

"I hope so, although some are probably so wrapped up in themselves that they are not aware what they are really doing. We should all be aware of what we do and how it affects others."

"I try not to make anyone mad at me."

"That's a good idea, but at times you have to be you and you have to do what is important to you, and that may have consequences. You can always try to do it in a way that it does not hurt others. The best thing to do is not to act hastily. Think about what you are about to do, why you are doing it, and explore all of the options."

"I like that you don't talk to me like a kid."

He was going to tell her that for all she had told him she was really no longer a kid. "I like to think I am talking to you like a daughter."

Twenty-Two

It was Saturday, and Sadie left for town to pick up milk and some other groceries with Yancy's credit card. She was also going to shop for Christmas gifts for Sally. They had discussed it the night before and decided that there would only be gifts for the little girl and that they would make it a happy Christmas for her. Yancy liked Christmas, but being by himself all these years he had no reason to decorate for the holiday. As a boy, there was no Christmas at the home, but he would head for the Catholic grandparents to partake of the holiday spirit. He remembered that as a warm time, and the message of good will to men and peace on Earth was still relevant.

It was a cold and clear day. While Sadie was in town, Yancy, Sally, and Chap went into the woods to find and cut down a Christmas tree. They passed some good possibilities almost right away, although Yancy wanted this to be a real adventure for Sally so they went further into the woods. They were well bundled up for the cold, and even Chap had one of his sweaters on.

"There's a good one," Sally yelled out pointing to a majestic tree off by itself. It was just the right size and appeared so perfectly shaped one would believe that it had been trimmed.

"You picked a winner," Yancy agreed.

"It is going to be a good Christmas."

He nodded. "I expect so."

"I just know that Santa will find me here."

"I expect so."

Yancy cut the tree down and dragged it along on the trek home. Chap barked his support. Sally sang Jingle Bells, and Yancy was pleased to see her so happy.

Back at the house, Yancy propped the tree up on the porch to await Sadie's decision where it should be set up in the house. Yancy had no decorations, although in anticipation Sadie was going to pick up items to make their own decorations including popcorn to be strung around the tree.

Yancy made hot chocolate with marshmallows and they sat around the wood stove to finish warming up. "This is a successful day," he announced between sips of the brew.

"This is a fun day." Sally retorted.

"Fun is a major part of success."

"Mr. Yancy, I love you."

His heart was warmed. "Sally girl, I love you."

Twenty-Three

With Santa's presents for Sally secure in the trunk of Sadie's car, it became an engaging treat to decorate the home for Christmas. After the tree was placed, decorations made and put on the tree, Yancy, Sally, and Chap ventured back to the woods to collect greenery to place inside and outside the house. It was nearly dark by the time they got back, a wheel barrow piled high with greenery.

Sally was exhausted and went to sleep right after supper. A bitter cold wind howled outside as Sadie and Yancy moved chairs close to the wood stove. Chap had gone in the bedroom with Sally but once he knew she was asleep he came out to lay by the stove. A quiet contentment shrouded the group.

"I can't adequately describe how I feel to see Sally so happy. I was thinking there would never be any full happiness in our lives." Sadie's voice trailed off as if she wanted to say more but thought better of it.

"There are some images better seen than described. Her happiness is nearly contagious. It has been a long time since I have felt that kind of euphoria."

"How am I ever going to thank you enough for what you are doing for us?"

"There is no need to do that. Again, the scene says it all."

There was a captivating smoothness to her voice that he had not been fully aware of. "It surprises me how happiness can be found in the simple things. The effort to make life more complicated is not worth it."

"There are many people who might not agree with that. I opted for a simple life because I thought it would help me with the writing. I underestimated it all. It has had an impact on the writing, but the peace and quiet I have here soothes my entire being. Walking in the woods with Sally and Chap was edifying as well as entertaining. It all boils down to instead of life making us we need to make life."

"An easy lesson to learn although hard to do."

"Perhaps. It may take longer in some instances than many people have patience for."

"My incentive is to get back to a place where Sally and I are not afraid, not timid about being happy or feeling guilty about it. You mentioned family secrets. Are you still in a dark place?"

"Yes, I am, but it is of my own making. I feel I need to be there to absorb its full significance and to write about it."

"After you finish the book, do you think you will be better?"

"Honestly, I don't know. I hope so. I would like my final years to be a calm after the storm."

"Is there anything Sally and I can do to help?"

"You already are."

Twenty-Four

7

Casey received a much warmer greeting from Lee the next time they met. She even smiled. "Hello, Mr. Casey. I like your tie."

"Howdy, Lee. The tie helps to keep my chin up." He did not get the laugh he anticipated. "You are looking good yourself." Her hair was neatly combed, and her jeans were new looking.

They sat next to each other and talked for awhile about the weather, how crowded and noisy the school was, and other small talk. Then she told him about the flute. Her talent in playing that instrument had gotten her into this prestigious school. In the fourth grade, an array of musical instruments was offered to students to try and take home for the weekend. She knew nothing about music or instruments but was intrigued by the flute, mainly because it was small and she was small for her age even then. She was fascinated by it, and as soon as she figured out how to blow into it, the magic began. She mastered it in no time without lessons, and discovered she had a keen ear for music.

There was a distinct shining in her eyes when she talked about the flute. "The flute is my soul. It takes me to a far better place than here. There are no people and no rules."

"What do you picture your future with the flute?"

"I want to play in an orchestra."

"There will be people and rules."

"Musicians are not ordinary people and rules about music are not rules."

"What are they?"

"I don't know what to call them but they are not rules."

"So, the flute is your lifeline?"

"Sure. What is yours?"

"I have yet to find one."

"What is it like to be a lawyer?"

"It is not a lifeline. It is a means to an end."

"What does that mean?"

"A way to earn money to buy the luxuries and conveniences that are here today and gone tomorrow."

"Do all lawyers talk such nonsense?"

"Not all, only those who look beyond what they have to do to what they want to do. You are fortunate to know what you want to do."

"The way I see it it's the only option I have to make any kind of future for myself."

"Does your future only include yourself?"

"I have no boyfriend if that is what you mean. Marriage and a family is nothing I think about."

"You might later on. What about your mother?"

"I don't feel anything for her."

"That's too bad."

"She doesn't really care about me. She doesn't like my music."

"Have you talked to her about it?"

"I have tried. She lives only in practical terms, only what she needs in her world."

"Are you in the school orchestra?"

"Yeah."

"Do they have concerts?"

"Yeah."

"I would like to come to the next one. Will you let me know when it is?"

"Sure."

"Does your mother come?"

"No."

"Maybe I can talk to her and she can go with me."

"I'd believe that when I see it."

"For a youngster you should have more faith in that things may work out the way you would like them to."

"I would believe it if I can see it."

"Maybe I can make you see it."

"Lots of luck."

"Will you play the flute for me before that?"

"Yeah." She kept looking away.

"Do I make you feel uncomfortable?"

"A bit. I don't know what to say to you or what you want me to say."

"I don't want you to say anything except what you want to say. I don't expect anything from you just as you should not expect anything from me except somebody to talk to and somebody who will listen to what you have to say. We are just getting to know each other. As I told you this is all new to me as well. Let's just see how it all plays out. There is a piece of classical music that you probably know about, called 'The Unfinished Symphony.' This will be our unfinished symphony. Can you relate to that?"

"I am not sure I can handle it."

"We can end this, I suppose, any time you want to, and you

can request a different father."

She was quiet for a moment. "No, I like you."

"I like you as well. Maybe we can finish a symphony together."

Twenty-Five

Sally dragged Sadie out of bed before dawn on Christmas morning. "Santa's been here!"

In anticipation of the forthcoming major commotion, Yancy was already up and sipping his coffee in the kitchen. He filled up a cup for Sadie.

With wrappings flung in all directions amidst squeals of delight, if one blinked at the scene the event would have been missed. Sally was totally absorbed in the gifts, especially the puzzles and books which she enjoys so much. Yancy figured breakfast would be delayed as eating was probably the last thing she might be interested in. He sat at the kitchen table with Sadie as they watched the spectacle by the tree.

"Another happy moment," Sadie uttered while sipping the coffee. "It has been a long time coming, but the happy times are multiplying. I think it will be some time yet before she is fully adjusted to and accepts happy times as a natural part of life. Bad memories cloud perception."

"For you more than for her. I know little about children, but I suspect they are more resilient than we think."

"Certainly more resilient than I am. I hate feeling sorry for myself, but I can't help it."

"It is better than keeping it bottled up."

"At least I don't depress others if I keep it to myself. I don't want you to feel sorry for me."

"We are family now. Comes with the territory."

"Were you ever married?"

"Yes, twice, and briefly I might add."

"What happened?"

"To make a long story short, I could not adapt to it and back then I was, I admit, very difficult to put up with. I may still be that way although I think I have mellowed quite a bit over the years. Time, as you will hopefully discover, settles our most restless spirit."

"You are easy to live with. I am the basket case and Sally extremely fragile. That is where hard to live with comes in."

"Justification for behavior is reason enough. And, not all justifications need to be explained. I feel you do not give yourself enough credit. You both are relatively easy to live with and also enjoyable to have around."

"I think you are just saying that because you are stuck with us."

"Believe me, I am not that nice. When one is old telling things as they are is the kind of honesty that would be even more beneficial if it took hold in the younger years."

"I don't consider you old."

"Some facts speak for themselves."

She grinned. "I didn't know facts could talk."

Another surprising feature. She was showing him that beneath the crust created by events there was a keen sense of humor. Another lesson that Yancy digested over the years is that it is easier to navigate over the swells of angry seas if one has a sense of humor. Not necessarily to laugh things away but to help absorb the shock waves. He would try to cultivate that in Sally. Growing up with a sense of humor is far better than developing it later on. It dawned on him that his story development making Casey a father figure with Lee was the same imprimatur for him. He smiled at the thought. Thought dawning can lead to physical manifestations.

Sadie thought he was smiling at her last remark. "A delayed reaction?"

"Old folks are glad for any reaction at all."

Twenty-Six

Later in the day, Sadie and Sally went to Millie's house for a traditional Christmas meal. Yancy had again declined an invitation to join them feigning matters that he needed to tend to. That left him alone to have the extra side dishes that Sadie left behind for him and to deal with his meandering thoughts.

It is not always a good thing to leave an author alone with his thoughts. A thought can be a dead end venture, or it can be an endless voyage, or it can be anywhere in between. Rereading the recitation in the manuscript of the dark secrets of his family depressed him mainly because there was much he could have done and should have done to allay the dire results. He was realistic enough to accept the fact that it was now far too late to change any of it. Yet, it was still emotionally draining, and it gave him an insight into Sadie's feelings. Perhaps, the house might be considered a hospital for the emotionally wounded.

Where does he go from here? What will happen to Casey? If he wanted to stop beating up on himself, he should probably do the same for Casey. In the broader philosophical realm he needed to consider if there was enough remaining of his basic being after all of the years that the secrets had torn him apart to make anything worthwhile. Would or could an opportunity to do a right offset any of the wrongs of the past in whole or in part? Certainly, a difficult situation for an author to deal with in his writing. Perhaps, an imponderable dilemma for him personally.

The other thought that had been brewing and was now taking a strong hold on any plan for a future was had he been unwittingly making life more complicated than it really needed to be? Had he been doing that as a form of self-punishment? It was truly a sobering contemplation. All of the years that he had deprived himself of the so-called pleasures of life could aptly be described as a waste. Should he have worked harder on the marriages and pursued having a family as well as establishing warm and lasting memories? If he had children, perhaps he would not have gotten to the point where because of the presence of Sadie and Sally he would not have to speculate what it would have been like.

He liked to believe that all of these mental deliberations would lead to better writing. After so many books and so many years, the mind stagnates. Maybe, these thoughts and a thorough self-analysis would serve as a shot in the arm and, hopefully, from arm to pen. Of course, there was no certainty in the value and outcome of thoughts. A lack of certainty might be a form of excitement for an old man whose otherwise placid life was getting him nowhere. It sure sounded like a form of fantasy to dream about and not to be lived.

A STORM WITHIN

Twenty-Seven

Early the next morning as Sally was munching on a bowl of cereal with the last of the milk supply, before finishing she put her spoon down and said in a hushed whisper so as not to awaken her mother, "Do you think I am pretty?"

It was not the kind of question he was prepared for, and he surmised that there would be few questions from an inquisitive child that he would be able to anticipate. "I don't think you are pretty. I know you are pretty."

"How do you know that?"

"I have no children of my own as you know, but when I was in New York I saw lots of little girls on the street, in stores, or on the subway, and compared to them you are very pretty."

"What makes me pretty?"

"Well, for those people hung up on looks, you have perfect features. Your head is the right shape, all the features of your face are in the right place and perfect. Your ears match and do not stick out; your nose is not too large or too small; your lips not too thin or too fat; and your eyes are clear and dazzling."

"What is dazzling?"

"So sparkly that they knock my socks off."

She giggled. "The way you talk, you must be a writer."

He smiled. Maybe, he would not have to show her how to have a sense of humor after all. "And, I will tell you something that writers know very well. It does not really make any difference what a person looks like on the outside. Beauty comes from within."

"What does that mean?"

"If a person is kind, caring, warm, and loving, then that person is truly beautiful. You are beautiful inside and outside."

"So are you, Mr. Yancy. That's why I know I love you."

"And I love you dearly, little Sally."

Later in the day when Yancy was alone with Sadie, he told her about the morning conversation. Its significance had lingered with him.

Sadie seemed despondent. "The cruelty of her father had no limits. He often called her an ugly brat. He told her repeatedly that nobody would ever like her because she was ugly and stupid. He would berate her for anything she did well." Tears formed in her eyes and her shoulders sagged perceptively. "Then he would beat her and tell her that ugly girls deserve to be beaten. He was a beast, a monster. I finally took Sally and we went to the shelter for women to escape from him. I swore he would never lay another hand on her or me either. I wonder if she will ever forgive me for letting it go on far longer than it should have."

Yancy put his arm around her shoulders and she lay her head on his chest. "I am sure she has already forgiven you, although it was not your fault. She looks at you with loving eyes that brim over with forgiveness."

"I hope that is true. The bigger task is for me to forgive myself."

"As I said, none of that was your fault. As I know all too well, there are times we get trapped in circumstances which later on we tell ourselves should never have happened, but at the time it might have been so overwhelming that it was too early or too difficult to make any reasonable choices."

Sadie spoke between sobs, "You are a kind and wonderful man."

"I haven't always been that way, I am afraid. As I said before, I have mellowed through no special effort on my part. That new found mellowness is bolstered because I sense it is what you need now."

"Not just now. It is the only possible future that I can see for us."

"I will do my best to help."

She hugged him with earnest. "I know you will."

Twenty-Eight

8

Casey knew it was a good sign when he entered the school room and Lee was holding her flute. A broad smile accompanied the greeting. "I am going to play for you."

"I had a feeling that today was going to be a special day."

He sat down next to her and the magic began. The flute came alive with sounds ranging from majestic to serene as the music dictated. He did not know much about music or instruments, but there was no doubt she was a master performer as he listened spellbound by the captivating sound. When she finished and put the flute down on the table, he patted the back of her hand and bellowed, "Bravo!"

"Did you really like it?"

"For sure, double. You are one gifted young lady. Thank you for sharing your love with me."

"I am happy you liked it." She was silent for a moment. "I want to ask you something personal."

"That's fine."

"Do you think I am plain looking?"

It was not a question that he was prepared for, so it took him a moment to respond. "What makes you think you are plain looking?"

"By the lockers this morning, the girls told me that is what Jack

Cassidy said."

"Who is Jack Cassidy?"

"The most popular boy in the school."

"That does not make him a good judge of character or anything else for that matter. And do you really care what he thinks?"

"Not really, I guess."

"You are darned right about that. Do you think you are plain looking?"

"Never really thought about it until now. I am not beautiful, I know that."

"What is the benefit of being beautiful?"

"I suppose it makes people popular."

"Hogwash. Do you think I am plain looking?"

"It doesn't matter for boys."

"It doesn't matter for girls either. We are all plain looking because looks don't really matter. Being happy with who you are and what you do is what counts. That is what makes you beautiful to yourself and your personality if genuine, caring, warm, and loving is what makes you beautiful to others. There is a very old saying that beauty is in the eye of the beholder. Where one person may see ugly another may see it as beauty. I see great beauty in you. You have all of the best qualities, and when you play the flute you're magnificent."

"All of that?"

"I'm just getting started. One who is beautiful on the inside is beautiful on the outside. Don't ever let looks be a criteria that you want others to judge you by, and for you to consider as the value for others. If you be a friend or make a friend, let loyalty, understanding, and compassion be the true substance of it all."

She smiled. "Wow, I really did get you started."

"Yes, you did."

"I wish you were a teacher at the school."

"Won't happen."

"How about being my publicity manager?"

"That is possible."

"Better than that, how would you like to be my father?"

Twenty-Nine

So, here he was as himself and as Casey at a crossroads. Does he go on brooding and be dominated by his past, or does he let the current developments lead him in a different direction? Is that what he should do for Sadie, Sally, and Lee? Did he deserve a change in the course of his life? If so, would he be able to adapt to it? It would also mean a major shift in the motive for writing the book. It was intended to be a catharsis, not a form of redemption.

There was definitely a shift in his thoughts and feelings from inside to outside. The three females needed him, not so much for himself as for what he represented. He was a symbol of security and hope. He had never experienced being truly needed by somebody. Sure, he was needed by his brother and his father, but that was different. The brother needed financial support, and his father needed him to bolster his endurance in light of the frustration and exasperation he was undergoing. Now, he was needed for love and guidance.

As the writer, he could rationalize by having it both ways. By reciting the deep dark family secrets he had already bared his soul. Even with a fictionalized setting, they were in effect no longer secrets. Mission accomplished in a way, clearing a path for other vicissitudes of life. Screams in the wind no longer had to be answered. It would be as if a beacon of light from a lighthouse could pierce the darkness and give him direction.

He could also rationalize that in his closing days he deserved some peace and happiness. A lesson he was learning late in life is that happiness can take various forms and come in different ways. One notable way is by doing for others. He should not deny that as a form of penance. Another lesson growing in his heart was that it is easy to love, and that to love can be very rewarding.

An additional dilemma was whether to just let it all play out or should he be an active participant in the shaping of forthcoming events. As an author, he was accustomed to fulfilling schemes promoted by the characters he was writing about. To do that for himself might take more from him than he was capable to give. One thing for sure, once he set out in a new direction all of those lingering questions would be answered. It would remain to be seen if he would be satisfied with the answers.

Thirty

There was a good deal of snow and many of the days with bitterly cold winds over the next month. They were pretty much confined to the house. Sally was involved with the schooling and with the puzzles and books she received from Santa. Chap was her constant companion. Sadie finished reading four more of Yancy's books, and she had pointed comments on each which resulted in extended discussions of the scope and vagaries of life.

Yancy did not get much writing done, although his mind was in overdrive. For a man who a short time ago rarely thought about the future other than dying, his mind led him to many possibilities. The end of secrets and the start of new adventures was something to dream about, perhaps nothing to write about. Yet, he suspected that as it unfolded for him he needed to reflect it in Casey.

At one of their breakfast sessions, all of a sudden Sally asked him, "What is going to happen to me?"

He was sorry Sadie was still asleep because he did not really know the best way to respond. "What do you want to happen to you?"

"I want to stay here with Chap."

"Anything else?"

"I don't want to be with any grownups or children."

"What about your mother?"

"She's here."

"What about me?"

"You, too."

"Wouldn't it be nice to play with other children?"

"No."

"They might have dogs."

"They still may be mean."

"Not all of them."

"How would I know which ones are not mean?"

"You can watch how they treat their dogs. Might be fun to find out."

"Maybe, some day. Not now."

"It can be fun and bring happy times to have a friend your own age. They may like to do puzzles, build snowmen, and take walks in the woods. If you decide to run through the woods, they can run with you. Your mom and I can't run much anymore. They might like sgetties also. You could play with their dogs and they can play with Chap."

She was silent, and he sensed she was soaking in the images he had portrayed. Children, he firmly believed, are like fertile fields. You can plant seeds and a bountiful harvest will emerge eventually. He would have guessed that when she did respond it would be a question. "Can that really happen?"

"Yes, little, girl, it really can happen."

Later, when Yancy related the discussion to Sadie, he suggested that when they make their next trip to town they might stop at the animal shelter. Sally might enjoy looking at the dogs, and there just might be children there with their families looking to adopt a dog. If that did not work, he had to take Chap to the veterinarian in town in the Spring for his annual checkup. He could try to arrange a time with the receptionist there, Harriet, to make the appointment to coincide with a visit by a girl around eleven who with her parents would be there with their dog. Sadie liked the ideas. She offered that if those did not work out, she might go to the school and talk with the teacher of the eleven-year-old class to work out something. She was anxious to get Sadie in social situations knowing it would help in the healing process. Yancy added that such an idea could work for her as well. She grimaced. "I'm not ready."

Thirty-One

9

It was evident that Lee had paid extra attention to her appearance. Her hair was neatly combed with not a strand out of place, and there was a hint of makeup on her face. They talked for awhile about school, the weather, and programs on television. Her look turned serious. "I have been thinking about my future ever since you asked me about it. I have no idea what to expect or what will happen to me."

"Besides playing the flute in an orchestra, what would you like to happen to you?"

She was silent although she stared at him steadily. "I don't know. I am afraid to think about it."

"Why? To dream and hope for a future filled with accomplishments is nothing to fear or even dread."

"This is serious."

"Yes, it is."

"I don't believe in dreams. It is another way of being hurt. I want to be realistic."

"A line from one of the songs in the musical South Pacific states that if you don't have a dream how do you expect a dream to come true. We all need to dream to strive for our future."

"Do you ever have good dreams?"

"Older people are restricted by time for their dreams. Yet, because of you I have a dream I never thought I would have."

"What is that?"

"I have a dream about a young girl I care enough about to guide her on the road of her dreams."

He could tell that he had hit a responsive chord in her thought processes and emotional turmoil. "How do I know if I can trust you?"

"The same way that I will know I can trust you. We try it and see what happens. There is a risk in all personal actions and reactions, and all you can do is try your best and hope that the rewards will make it all worthwhile."

She was silent again for a moment. "I try not to do more than I know I can get done or to hope for more than I can expect because I can't handle disappointment."

"Disappointment is part of life. All efforts cannot be successful all of the time. I think you are stronger than you give yourself credit for. You can bounce back from any disappointment, and even learn from it so that the next effort is better planned."

She shrugged her shoulders and there was a definite dejection in her voice. "I am weaker than you make me out to be."

"I say if you give it a chance you will surprise yourself."

There was a hint of a smile on the thin lips. "Maybe."

He got up to leave and he felt it was a good talk. She surprised him by hugging him and he wrapped his arms around the thin frame to acknowledge her gesture. Both were more hopeful than they were before.

Thirty-Two

10

That night as Casey sat at the desk he had in the living room of his apartment, he had intended to work on the papers he had brought home from the office. His mind, however, ran in a different direction. He could still sense Lee's hug, and he wondered if that, as well as his desire to be there for her to infuse the prospect of an emotionally satisfactory life, could offset the consuming effects of the deep dark family secrets.

The deep dark family secrets were the raging personal storm in his soul. It had been growing in intensity until now, consuming any efforts or chances for contented living. He had been so absorbed by the guilt of his role in those haunting events that he did not give any thought to a future where the effects might be pushed aside for anything new or different. Now, he wondered whether Lee would wind up doing more for him than he was going to do for her.

For so many years he had been preoccupied with the secrets, perplexed about anything that could be done to alleviate the pain. A subtle shift of attention away from himself to a meandering youngster eased his pain to the extent that he was able to think of something else besides his complicity in the demise of his family. Would it be enough to give him some peace in the closing days of his life? He was planning to retire next year, and he had given little thought as to what he might do or where he might go. By emphasizing to Lee that she should dream about a future, perhaps that same advice could be true for him. Rather than dealing totally with a storm in his heart and mind, he might focus on the aftermath. Beyond a storm there is a calm clearing where he might emerge with a new outlook and a positive prospect. Could he leave the shadows behind to bask in a new light? Did he even deserve to think in such terms?

Thirty-Three

Spring was late in arriving, and as if Nature wanted to compensate for the delay Summer came early. A low key routine brought a basic calm to the household. Sally fought the tranquility as only a high-spirited rebellious youth could. She resisted in highly charged terms all efforts to find a friend for her. Her comfort was with Chap, and Sadie did not want to push any limits to fully test the existing fragility of the little girl. She knew she had to be patient with her. Time is still the best healer.

Sadie seemed to be making better progress in putting herself back together. She even freely talked one evening about her parents. Those folks were aloof and distant to her as well as Millie, offering little emotional support in the growing years. They both died from COVID-19 during the height of the pandemic and before a vaccine was available. Before that Millie had met George, and marriage to an older farmer living in rural Vermont appeared to be her best escape route from a stale and unpromising life. Sadie had met her future husband at a party at the newspaper she was working for, and his jovial behavior and stable economic position enticed her into marriage. She should have been more wary and had greater perception to guard against a volatile future, but throwing caution to the wind comes easy for a young woman desperate for love and a family. Later she learned the hard way that such a wind can be dangerous and can carry one to anywhere or nowhere.

Sadie started to receive the support payments for Sally on a regular basis. She offered to turn the money over to Yancy although he would not take it. It was agreed that she would buy the groceries.

One day in the dwindling days of the Summer, Sadie was awakened by Sally shaking her. At first, she thought that maybe the little girl was anxious to go that day to the Education Building where they planned to pick up the home schooling materials for the forthcoming school year. "Mr. Yancy won't wake up."

Sadie nearly collapsed finding that Yancy had died in his sleep. As if Chap knew, he lay by Yancy's side on the bed. He would not move and Sadie had to carry him away. As if Yancy suspected that something might happen to him, prominently placed on his writing station was a printed copy of the unfinished manuscript and his Last Will and Testament. The house as well as all his money and possessions were left to Sadie. Chap was left to Sally. The document was witnessed by Millie and George, and Sadie wondered when Yancy must have stopped by their house to have them do the signing.

Sadie moved into Yancy's room so that Sally could have a room to herself. She left Yancy's writing station just as it was, a permanent reminder of and tribute to the force that had pulled her from the deep emotional depths and lifted her up so that her face was in the sun.

Sadie had a small area cleared behind the house. Yancy was buried there, and before the cold weather set in she planted flowers all around the spot. She regretted not ever telling him that she loved him, although he must have sensed it. He never told her he loved her as he often stated to Sally, but she knew he did because of his caring actions and attitude. Leaving everything he had to her was further confirmation.

It took her a month before she could bring herself to read the manuscript. It made her cry, tears that she had withheld until then. There was no way to tell just how much of the family history was true, although she suspected that it was all or mostly true. Through their many talks she had concluded that Yancy was a deeply troubled man. The move to this desolate life was not really because of his writing. He had withdrawn from life as a way of handling his guilt. She only hoped that she and Sally had given him some comfort in his final days. She wished she had done more. It was an eye-opening revelation that she was not the only person who had to deal with a family horror. She swore to herself that his memory would make her even stronger to deal with her ordeal and to meet and conquer all obstacles in life for her and Sally. Yancy was her hero.

Sadie decided that they would make their life there. The house was comfortable, private, and secure. It had the feeling of home. Living in the country was also satisfactory. It was serene and pleasing, and having Millie close by was a plus. She smiled recalling Yancy's pronouncement that time stands still on a country road. The future might bring major changes, but for the moment she wanted to preserve this promising present. She had a marker made and placed it by Yancy's grave. It read:

HERE LIES A KIND, GENTLE,
AND LOVING MAN —

SYMBOLIC FATHER AND GRANDFATHER,
LOVED IN RETURN —

REST IN DESERVED PEACE

Thirty-Four

Sadie went often to the back of the house and would sit on the bench she had put by Yancy's grave. She would talk to him as if he was listening intently. Mainly, she would detail her thoughts, feelings, and plans. The dialogue would be ended each time by an expression of her gratitude and love for him. He was her father in death as he had become in life.

On the first anniversary of Yancy's death, Sadie lingered for a long time by the grave. She sat on the bench and expounded on all that had happened over the year. Sally had come out of her shell and had become adjusted to friends and a full and active life as a youngster. Sadie had talked to a teacher at the school who had told her about Kate Yearling, a delightful, outgoing, and well adjusted eleven year old girl with a dog. She gave her the mother's telephone number, and when Sadie telephoned Glinnis Yearling and told her all about the situation, Glinnis was quite willing to help out. They arranged for a meeting between the girls and their dogs at a park just outside of town, and that naturally eased into a friendship that grew rapidly. Visits at their respective homes were frequent and enjoyable. The girls turned twelve one week apart and a big joint birthday party at Glinnis' house was a truly special event as Sally intermingled with all of the children invited for the occasion. Sally became so involved in all of these new experiences that she was the one who proposed she go to the public school the next year as she would be in Kate's class.

Sadie and Glinnis also became close during all of the contact times, and that easily became a meaningful friendship. It was a calm transition for Sadie from a wary and reserved person to one who could share confidences with another and be comfortable in social situations.

To keep traditions going, at Christmas Sadie, Sally, and Chap went deep into the woods to cut a tree, and they selected one they thought Yancy would have liked. Sally recounted the earlier time with Yancy and how much she loved being with him. Sadie's voice was the only sound in the silence. "Your lingering loving presence is constantly felt in the house and our lives, and it fortifies our day-to-day living. That will be the way it is always."

Sadie then stood up and stared down at the grave. "Yancy, dearest man, I tell you now as I should have when you were here − I love you. I should have done more to bring you some happiness to offset even a little of the tragedy of your life. I should have done it for all of your efforts to do that for us. I hope you will not think me too presumptuous, but I want to do it for you now. The only way I can do that is by doing it for Casey. Since I will have plenty of time while Sally is in school, I am going to finish writing your book."

Thirty-Five

11

The next time Casey met with Lee they hugged without hesitation. She gave him two tickets to the school orchestra concert to be held three weeks from Saturday night in the school auditorium. "Are you still going to try and talk my mother into going?"

"I will make it so appealing she won't be able to say no."

"I don't think it will work, and I don't believe in miracles."

"Write out your address and telephone number on a sheet of paper, and I will take it from there. What is your mother's name?"

She wrote out the information for him. "Her name is Celia. And you should know we live in a hell hole."

"That is probably all she can afford." He thought about his own large apartment in the high rent district. He had received a bargain for the three-bedroom apartment through the law firm. It was much more space than he wanted, but he figured he better grab it since at the time he did not know what the future was going to be with his father. If he failed, Casey did not want to put him in a home. This way he would have room for him as well as for a live-in nurse if that was the case.

"People bang on the walls when I play the flute. They think it is a terrible noise."

"You know better than to let anything sway you from your passion."

"I am going to tell you something I have never told anyone else." Her look was far off.

"That is what fathers are for I am beginning to learn."

"I always wanted a dog."

"Funny you should mention that. I thought about that myself when I was a boy, but the building we were in did not allow pets, and I didn't dare mention it."

She shrugged her shoulders. "Same here. I just always thought it would be nice to have a dog who would love me no matter what."

"Parents do that."

"I wouldn't know."

"I am sure your mother does."

"As I told you, she doesn't show it."

Before he said it, Casey fully realized that he already loved this little girl. The surprise was that in spite of the ghosts rattling around in his heart and mind, it was easy to love a child. "I am your father now. I love you."

He hugged her and she stayed in his arms. "I love you, too."

Thirty-Six

12

Casey waited until the following afternoon to telephone Celia. Since she worked the night shift at the diner she probably slept in the mornings. He wanted to speak to her while Lee was still at school.

"Hello."

"Celia?"

"Yes."

"I am Casey Trumbeaux. I am Lee's surrogate dad in the program at the school."

Her voice was not as harsh as he thought it might be. In fact, it was rather soothing. "I know who you are. Lee talks about you all the time."

"I talk about her as well. She is a delight."

"Usually, she hardy talks to me."

"That doesn't mean she will not. You need to work at it. Music is her driving force, and you need to respect and encourage that. That is the place you two must meet."

"I know nothing about music."

"I don't either, but that does not mean you can't appreciate it. She has great talent. If you let her share it with you, you will be surprised how much there will be to talk about."

"I wouldn't know how to begin to do that."

"That is why I am calling you. The school orchestra is giving a concert in the school auditorium in three weeks. If you go to it and cheer her on, she will know that you are interested not only in her music but also in her. It will bring you closer together."

"I work nights."

"Saturday night?"

"Not the weekends."

"Good, the concert is Saturday night. I would like you to go with me."

She did not respond right away. "I am not sure."

"Oh, come on. We can make it a fun time for her as well as for you. After the concert, we can take Lee out for a pizza or ice cream. It can be a time for you to share with her what she loves."

Another brief silence. "I would like to do it, but I am not sure about it."

"I don't have a car, but I will pick you up in a taxi, and we can go together. I already have the tickets. There will be no fussing, no expectancies, and no hassles. It will be just a natural and enjoyable night out to see your daughter perform and to give her a good time. Do it for her."

"Alright."

Thirty-Seven

13

"You could have knocked me out with a sheet of music," Lee offered in a hushed tone after she hugged him. "She said you invited her to the concert and she agreed to go. She even went to her closet to see if the one dress she has still fits. I don't know how you talked her into it, but I am glad you did. She even said you are as nice as I have said you are."

"That's because I am."

"I know that. Now she knows it, too. She even said you were going to take us out after the concert. She hasn't done anything like that for as long as I can remember."

"Maybe, a little dream you might have is coming true. Perhaps, even a little dream she may have had is also materializing."

"Are you sure you are for real?"

"As real as it all can be, certainly as real as it could be."

"You are more than a lawyer. You are a magician."

He laughed, and it struck him that he had not laughed in a long time. "Perhaps, the magic is just beginning."

"Do you know what else? When she was telling me all of this she was looking directly into my eyes. Then, she talked about a whole bunch of things and all I could do was smile and feel your influence on our lives. How can I thank you for what you are doing?"

"No need for that as I am enjoying it all. At times all it takes is a subtle nudge to get things moving in the right direction or to make new paths."

"There you go again with all that lawyer nonsense, but I guess it is part of your magic so I will not question it even if I do not understand it."

"I will tell you a truism. You will understand it as you live it. What it really means is that I will not be your father anymore."

She shouted out, "What?"

I am destined to be your mother's father. "I am going to be your grandfather."

Thirty-Eight

14

When Lee described she lived in a hell hole, that may have been an understatement. The building was in a run down part of the city, and it was dilapidated and maintained poorly, if at all. The lobby was small and shabby, the hallways dark and dingy, and the smell of mold and mildew was prevalent. There was no elevator, and Casey had to walk up three flights of dark stairs to get to the apartment. When Celia opened the door to his knocking, the apartment was no better. He looked past her to see the meager possessions and faded furniture in a dimly lit living room with paint peeling off the walls.

Celia was a breath of fresh air. A petite woman greeted him with a warm smile, and he was struck by the same long black hair and piercing black eyes that enhanced Lee's appearance. Casey guessed that she must have been very pretty when she was younger, and the face now reflected some hard living and disappointing times. The smile revealed uneven and some missing teeth. The outdated green dress hung loosely on the overly skinny body.

They went down to the waiting taxi. On the ride over to the school, the conversation was pleasant. Celia seemed nervous and avoided talking about herself, although she described her limited life with Lee. She emphasized their struggling existence, and without providing details mentioned the abuse they had suffered by her husband. Casey could, of course, recognize and sympathize with the dark secrets that loomed beyond her words. Her hands appeared to shake slightly, and he noticed the long tapered fingers and guessed there might have been other musicians in the family history. Her voice was as smooth and calming as it was on the telephone. His initial assessment was that this was once a vibrant woman whose flame had been extinguished and whose goodness was bottled up.

While they waited in their seats for the concert to begin, Celia kept looking at the people around them. Her tone was low and the words forced. "I don't belong here."

Casey looked into those captivating black eyes. "Yes, you very much do. You are as good as any of them, and you are about to witness the remarkable achievement of your daughter which carries you both far above where you are and where you were and to a place of high esteem."

A half of a smile appeared on the thin lips. "I see why Lee adores you. You bolster even those who are down and out."

"She is far from down and out. Her talent is extreme. Her wonderful and perceptive feelings about life will bring her happiness and success. Why shouldn't the same be possible for you?"

There was a perceptible slump of the body. "Because reality tells me there is no chance for me. You see how we live, and I work hard for every penny I make. There is no chance for a better life and I accept that as my fate." A tear formed at the corner of one of the black eyes. "I try to be there for her, but the reality of it prevents me from succeeding. I can't even look her in the eyes. I don't want to see the disappointment in them she has for me, and I don't want her to see the disappointment I have in myself. I am at a dead end. I know it. Being here and seeing all of this, I realize it even more."

"Celia, I try to emphasize to Lee that it is important to have dreams. Dreams mean hope. Hardship brings pain, there is no denying that, but you have treasures that you must let guide you. You have each other. You are healthy and have all of your senses. Lee has a bright future, and you can share in it. You have to be happy for her in it so that she can be happy in it. You are also entitled to have a dream of your own, and perhaps when you least expect it that dream may come true."

The tear slid down the wrinkled cheek. "Not for me."

The concert was wonderful, and Lee's position on the stage made it easy for Casey and Celia to watch her every move. Casey could tell that Celia was spellbound. Seeing her daughter in full action is quite different than hearing her practice and imagining a full orchestral sound.

After the concert, they waited for Lee in the lobby and then they walked down the street to a restaurant that was still open. They had ice cream sundaes, and talk and laughter came easily. Celia kept looking at Lee with pride and love in those searing black eyes. Casey knew that Lee sensed it, and she smiled when her mother repeatedly told her how wonderful her performance was.

Casey walked them up to their apartment, and when he said goodnight they both hugged him. As Celia withdrew from her hug, the voice was soft and warm, "Thank you, kind man. Thank you for a night I will never forget."

In the taxi on the ride back to his place, Casey fashioned the plan that had been brewing in his mind and heart. With such thoughts occupying so much of his attention, the ghosts of his past moved to the background and they were unusually silent.

Thirty-Nine

15

Casey was going to wait until Monday afternoon to present to Celia what he had in mind, but he was so wound up he called Sunday instead. He was a man on a mission.

"Hello," Celia answered.

"Celia, it is Casey. First, I wanted to thank you for making last night so enjoyable. You were wonderful company."

She hesitated, "We need to thank you over and over again. It was a good time all around. Lee is doing her homework. Do you want to speak to her?"

"No, I want to talk to you."

"Oh."

"I have something to offer to you, I don't expect you to answer it right away. I am a lonely man, old way before my time, and I am going to retire next year. I live in a comfortable building on the other side of the city. I have a three-bedroom apartment because I thought I might eventually have my parents living with me and to care for. They are gone now. The space is going to waste, and I sure would like to have company like a family here. That means you and Lee. Each of you would have a separate bedroom. I have a cleaning service come in once a week and that is expensive. Instead of them, you could take care of the place and do the shopping and cooking. I would pay you as a housekeeper the amount I have been paying the cleaning service, and you would have free room and board. You will have a comfortable and healthy place to be at, and I would have a family. I have no children of my own. Lee is already like a granddaughter, and that would make you like a daughter. I know this is much to throw out at you, but perhaps it can be a start for a dream for you. It would be real good for Lee. There are soundproof walls here so she can practice all she wants to, and she will be comfortable and secure. The harsh lives you have had can be offset here. I will make no demands of either of you. How does it all sound?

Celia was silent for a moment. "This is very kind of you, and I am sure you have thought it through. You don't know what you will get. We are both emotionally beat up and we would be a drag on your life."

"I doubt it. I look at it as being good for all of us."

"I will think about it. This comes as a surprise. It is very much appreciated that you think of us that way. I am sure Lee would love it, but I don't want her to be unrealistic. I just don 't know."

"I have said my piece. No pressure and no obligation. You have my number. Call me when you have made a decision. I have thought it all through and would not have offered if there was any doubt on my part."

"I will call you. Thank you, again. It is very generous of you."

Forty

16

Celia just sat there for a long time after she hung up on the telephone call with Casey. Was she just a witness to a miracle? Had Casey's encouragement last night for her to dream brought a dream and its fulfillment all at once?

A look back at her life brought tears to her eyes. From the poverty of her family in Mexico where she was the youngest of four children and coming to the United States when she was four only to suffer amidst a different kind of economic struggle as migrant workers in the California town they settled in. Her parents died poor and disheartened, and the oldest sister raised the family barely scraping along in the squalor that surrounded them. She recalled the constant blisters on her young hands and the visual and emotional recording of seemingly endless days of strenuous labor in blistering heat. There was no time for fun, no time for herself. She did not go to school, although that eldest sister taught her to read and write in English. At eighteen, when Ricardo Valesquez came from New York City to visit his brother in the town, she thought he was the answer to her prayers when he took an interest in her and offered to take her with him to New York City where he worked as a salesman. She hardly knew him, and knew nothing of what might be expected of her. She had heard of and seen abuse between men and women but just never related it to herself until it happened. She became pregnant with Lee, and discovered that her husband was a womanizer and a heavy drinker. He spent most of his money on women and at bars, and the substandard living conditions closed in on her. It was a cruel realization that she was really no better off than before. Ricardo's financial frustration and drinking led him to physically strike both Celia and the child, even more so when he came home very drunk. She had no choice but to endure and the very sap of her being was drained from her. There could be no thoughts of a tomorrow. To this day, she could not understand how or why a man would take out the self-making misery of his own life out on a helpless woman and child. Then, one day he was gone, and she figured he had run off with another woman or had been killed. The promise of hardship continued, even if its demands were different.

Along came Casey, and in a blink of an eye there appeared the opportunity for a promising tomorrow. The human traits of kindness and generosity which she had heard existed but had never experienced were suddenly presented to her. It was a dream if there ever was one.

Celia went to where Lee was doing her homework. She told her about Casey's proposal. With great animation Lee encouraged her mother to accept the offer. Her mother hugged her, and Lee could not remember when her mother had done that before. Celia telephoned Casey before he had any chance of changing his mind.

Forty-One

17

So, a rather unusual family unit was born. By all indications, it promised to be successful. The participants were going to do all they could to make it so.

Lee was excited to be able to pick out all of the furniture and decorations for her room. With the flute close by, her room was a domain to feel warm and secure against any ill winds that might stir up. It was a place in which she would dare to dream the kind of dreams Casey had said she might have. When Christmas came another dream was fulfilled. Casey gave her a small mixed terrier from the animal shelter. She named her Flute and the two became inseparable. Lee's greatest discovery was that there seemed to be no limit for the love that she felt for her new grandfather. He emerged at a time of probably her greatest need for stability and guidance, and she hung on each word he uttered and hugged him at every turn.

Even after months, Celia was still in a partial state of disbelief that she had finally found a home. She had thought she would never see the day where her mind and heart could relax. She felt pride caring for the apartment, doing the shopping, and preparing meals for Casey and Lee. It was the feeling of being needed that gave her the greatest satisfaction. She had a purpose in life, and that brought her closer than ever to her daughter. She would walk the dog for her when she was in school. Casey was able to get her a divorce from Ricardo based on abandonment, and Celia had the sense that she was now free. Little wonder that she had a love for this man who turned her life around. That also opened her mind, and she started to read books and would ask Casey to explain things to her. He also arranged for extensive dental work so that she would feel better about her appearance. With Casey's assistance she got involved in helping out at a woman's shelter in the city, and she was determined to help make life better for its residents as Casey had done for her.

Casey was probably the one in the family that emerged with the greatest reward. The discovery of his need and ability to love and be loved loosened most of the shackles of his past. Not believing he would ever be happy, he luxuriated in a state of true contentment and a sense of being needed. There was laughter in the apartment, and he would sit back with eyes closed when Lee would practice the flute to let the music reach the remnants of his soul. His past would always be there to be dealt with by his conscience. The ghosts would not go away although they could be quieted. The storm within will do no further damage. Along with his advice to others to dream, he was now able to do that for himself.

Forty-Two

Sadie turned off the master's computer at his work station when she finished printing out the addition to the book. She acknowledged to herself that her addition was not great prose, probably not even good writing at all. It would more than likely be categorized as amateurish. She could not write as well as he could, and she certainly did not have the command of vocabulary that he had possessed. All that did not deter her. Her purpose had been achieved by the writing, and that was all that mattered. It would not be published or even read by anyone else unless Sally wanted to do so when she was older. It was her testament to a man worthy of love and happiness. She had immortalized that by allowing the character he had created as his alter ego to find a modicum of contentment. The beasts of his past were not slain but were held at bay.

Sadie tied a red ribbon from the Christmas collection around the finished manuscript and put it on the work station which she would leave intact for as long as they were in the house as a shrine to him. She kissed the collected pages as she laid it down by the computer. No one could hear her, but she said it aloud anyway as it was her heart speaking. "With love, dearest father of mine. Your secrets are safe there with you. Sleep well, forever."